Lonesome Roads

Peter Crowther

*Introduction by
Graham Joyce*

*RazorBlade
Press*

Lonesome Roads

This book was first published in 1999 by
RazorBlade Press, 108 Habershon St, Splott, Cardiff,
CF2 1PQ.

"Forest Plains" (c) 1996 by Peter Crowther
"The Space Between the Lines" (c) 1998 by Peter Crowther
"Stand by" (c) 1999 by Peter Crowther
Introduction (c) 1999 by Graham Joyce

All rights reserved

Lonesome Roads is a work of collected fiction.
The characters and events described are imaginary and any
resemblance to people living or dead is purely
coincidental.

Designed and typeset by
RazorBlade Press

Printed and bound in the U.K

British Library in Publication Data.
A catalogue record for this book is available
from the British Library

ISBN 0-9531468 1-2.

Lonesome Roads

Introduction

by
Graham Joyce

In Pete Crowther's 'The Space Between The Lines' there is a character who can make comic-book panels come to life.

The story rocketed me back to the time when, aged seven, I was making a train journey from the Midlands to the north of England to visit my father's relations. On the platform, Dad asked me if I wanted a comic from the newsstand. I said yes, and he chose one for me.

I didn't open the comic until we were well underway and I wasn't entirely satisfied with his choice. When I'd said a 'comic' what I meant was one of the usual standbys: the *Dandy*, the *Beano*, the *Beezer* or the *Topper*. Comics that made you laugh... or at least chuckle. OK, sometimes you were lucky if they even managed to conjure up a smile, but fundamentally they were just little timekillers printed on thin, grey paper with ink that transferred to your thumbs. They were not supposed to open up new worlds.

This comic, casually tossed into my lap by my father that day, was something altogether different. To begin with it was clearly foreign in its conception and design. It carried alien advertisements for unfamiliar merchandise that was priced in dollars and it had dockets on which you should write your name, address and something called a zip-code. I recall asking my Dad what a zip-code was, exactly, quite liking the sound of it. He opened his eyes, minimally shook his head, and went back to sleep again. The comic, you see, was supposed to keep me quiet for the train journey, not encourage me to bother him with a lot of fool questions.

The comic in question was a *World of Boris Karloff* special edition. At least I think that's what it was called. Maybe it was *Boris Karloff's Strange World*

v

Lonesome Roads

or something like that. You know the formula. But at the time I'd never heard of Boris Karloff, yet there he was, quite a distinguished-looking but moody individual, his disembodied head topping and tailing five stories of the supernatural.

Man, they were spooky stories. I can remember them all as if I'd read them yesterday. One was about a South American dictator leading a double-life and determined to destroy his other self; another was about Tommyknockers (this was long before Stephen King) in an American mining disaster; a third was about a chair that hated women.

After that stuff you could never go back to the *Topper*. It was like you had gone through a door. I fell asleep on the train, and I even started dreaming about the Tommyknockers.

'The Space Between The Lines' — or the character who can bring the panel scenes to life — is a metaphor for all that. And that's what happens every time I read one of Pete's stories: I see a metaphor behind the narrative, and something strange rises out of the story, back-lit, rippling with catch-light, luminous at the bleed of the line, and I'm seven again and on a hurtling train with my nose in a comic that is a doorway.

Perhaps it's the strangeness, the originality of some of his ideas that does it. In this time of horror re-treads and recycled terrors, there is always something about a Pete Crowther story that takes a horror trope, gives it a sharp tug and pulls it into a brand new shape.

In 'Stand-By' the protagonist visits a medium who can bring his wife back from the dead. Nothing new about that, but get this: the revenant can't actually do anything. Can't speak, can't act, has to be led around from place to place. But it can sit in the corner looking like the original. It's such a chilling idea; far more so than if it could act, or re-appeared in a state of decomposition, or operated in standard spectre mode.

This is the great thing about these stories. They don't operate in standard mode.

In 'Forest Plains', a Native American nemesis-figure comes into a small town, equipped with preternatural olfactory powers, ready to literally sniff out the town's darkest secrets and lies. Again, the richness of the story lies in its capacity to suggest the extraordinary proximity of parallel worlds; and yet even as I use that tired phrase I realise its inaccuracy in the case of any of these tales. These are other worlds which actually dovetail into the contemporary in exhibitions of crafted jointing.

The point of intersection is always at the moment of emotional crisis or moral upheaval, and that's what makes these stories count. The horror or the terror or the exhibition of the fantastic — for want of other words — is an expression of psychic distress manifesting itself. These are not simply stories to while away a train journey.

Which brings me back to my favourite story here, 'The Space Between The Lines'. The subject matter is so original, and the growing excitement of the story is so well handled, you could easily be forgiven for not pausing to take a good look at the space between the lines, at the understated moral and emotional force of the story.

I read these tales and I'm back on that hurtling train again, with my nose between the covers. But this time the stories are for grown-ups, and new doors are being opened, and the excitement is undiminished.

Let me also tell you that Pete, in addition to being a writer and editor, is also a great collector within the genre. Perhaps that's why his stories have such original force — he won't settle for the ordinarily horrific or the hackneyed fantastic. Certainly, as a writer, I always dread him asking me what I'm working on or whether I'll write a story for one of his anthologies. He's quite likely to send me — in a genuine spirit of helpfulness, I should add — a photocopy of some obscure short story handling the same theme far

Lonesome Roads

better than I ever could manage.

Pete knows the field and he knows who has covered what ground before. Which is why you can rely on him to mint it all anew. Come to think of it, I must ask him if he knows about that Boris Karloff comic.

Graham Joyce
May 1999

Lonesome Roads

CONTENTS

Forest Plains
page 2

Standby
page 36

The Space Between the Lines
page 92

Forest Plains

All of the Indians are dead
(a good Indian is a dead Indian)
Or riding in motor cars
               Ernest Hemingway
               (from *Oklahoma*)

"What then is the American,
this new man?"
               Crevecoeur

(1)

The dead man drove his car through the ghosts of his people.

He saw their spirits hovering over the black top like heat shimmer or the tail ends of the morning haze that runs across the meadow in early summer, when the sun is still drying out the winter earth. When he got out of his car at a Mobil gas station twenty-three miles north of Kansas City, he could even smell them.

He rubbed his hands along his back, stretched and faced into the gentle breeze, sniffing. Alongside his head, flies and the occasional wasp buzzed by. Behind him, a screen door whined and then clanked twice. The sound of slurring feet approaching his back made him turn.

"Premium?" The old man reached for the nozzle without waiting for an answer and thrust it into the side of the Dodge. He had already started to squeeze the trigger.

"Premium'll do just fine." He turned back to face the wind and breathed in again, recalling the words of Chief Luther Standing Bear, passed through the generations. *The world was a library and its books were the stones, leaves, grass, brooks, and the birds and animals that shared, alike with us, the storms and blessings of the earth.*

"Smell anything?" The old man stooped over the Dodge, dutifully wiping spilled gasoline from a rusting fender as the traces of his words hung in the air like the wind on a wire fence. He was watching the dead man, watery eyes squinting into the sun.

The dead man breathed deep, pulling the air into his lungs.

Smell anything...

He smelled cheap supermarket fats, and frying eggs, steaks and sausages.

He smelled pancakes, syrups and coffee, some of it freshly made, some of it old now — old in coffee terms

— and losing its life warmth.

He smelled cigarettes — he identified eleven brands before giving up the game - and cologne, a handful of cheap perfumes and the faintest hint of prophylactic lubrication.

He smelled the fresh water of the Missouri River.

He smelled dirt and chemicals.

And, most of all, he smelled the past.

The old man's question swooped and dived amidst the gentle, regular ting of the gas pump as it fed the old Dodge. It ached to be answered and released. The dead man breathed deep again, filtering odours through the cloying smell of gasoline, and pulled in the prairie.

He smelled the Assiniboin and the Cree, the Massika and the Maudan, the Arikara and the Blackfoot. And many more besides. He smelled buffalo hides, skins of beaver, muskrat and lynx, some fox, a little weasel and mink.

He smelled tepee smoke and rat shit.

And then he smelled something sleazy. It hung on the wind like a trapped ribbon, swirling and dropping, but always returning to the same point. He closed his eyes and sniffed some more, short sniffs, concentrating on the unfamiliar scent. Then he recognised it. It was death and pain, sudden and brutal. The smell made the dead man gag and put his hand to his face.

Behind him, the old man replaced the gas nozzle and set to cleaning the windshield with a piece of gingham cloth, which he pulled out of his pants pocket. The cloth was filthy with grime and dust. The Cree Chief, Piapot once said: *The white man who is our agent is so stingy that he carries a linen rag in his pocket into which to blow his nose, for fear he might blow away something of value.* The dead man smiled and stared at the rag. Maybe there had even been a time when that piece of cloth had been just a part of a larger garment.

He concentrated, just for his own amusement.

It had been a long time for that piece of cloth, and

a lot of windshields and spilled gasoline, but it was there, buried beneath the grease and snot: the faint waft of young legs, feminine legs, the gentle, teasing odour of dawn-hair and pheromones.

He smiled to himself, pushing the smells back, away from him. "Breakfast," he said at last, the word springing out into the heat as though it had a life of its own.

"Huh?"

The dead man rubbed his stomach. "I smell breakfast. Know where I can chow down around here?"

The old man stepped back from the car, rubbed a grizzled beard that was more bush grass than meadow, and jammed the cloth into his pocket. The dead man saw a flash of coloured stripes through the old man's fly as it gaped open and then closed back up. And he caught the stench of urine and stale jism, crabs and shit. He turned away quickly and drank in the scents of the land again. It was worse than ever, his 'gift'. It was getting so that he couldn't stop from pulling them all in.

"Well," the old man said, telling it like a campfire story on the back of a long day and a shared bottle, "you go on along here a ways — mebbe eight, nine miles — you come to a fork: left, lemme see now... left is marked Railroad Crossing." The old man smiled. "That's all it is. That's all that's down there.

Right is where you need to go, town name of Forest Plains. Ain't much more'n a general store, an auto fix-it and a bar, but the store does an all-day breakfast that should set you up some." The old man chuckled and the dead man turned back to face him, his eyes asking the question. "Fact is," the old man said, still laughing, "they cook but the one meal but they do it all day. It can be any meal you want it to be. It'll be as good as any breakfast you ever had." He looked up at the sign measuring the time, and the dead man noticed that the old man did not wear a watch. "Be as good as any lunch you ever had,

5

too." The old man thought for a minute and then added, "Nice girl there. Indian." He smiled a superior smile, exposing blackened gaps in old bridgework, and nodded to the dead man. "Should make you feel right at home."

"Sounds fine to me," the dead man said and he turned his head to look up the road. The wrong-death smell was still there. "Forest Plains." He turned the words over in his mouth until they started to feel right. That was the place. He could feel it as well as smell it.

"That'll be sixteen-eighty-five for the gas."

The dead man pulled two crumpled bills from his jacket pocket, straightened them with his hand and then held them out. "There you go," he said "Twenty dollars. Keep it."

"Hey," the old man beamed, taking the bills and folding them into his pants pocket on top of the gingham cloth, with all of its ingrained history. "That's mighty kind of you. Mighty kind." His eyes twinkled his gratitude. Maybe now the old man was regretting the Indian crack.

"My pleasure." The dead man walked around to the driver's door.

"Nice auto," the man said, earning his tip.

"Was once," the dead man said. "Now it's like me, dead but it won't lie down. Dodge Royal, 1954." He rested his arm on the door and pointed his hand to the hood. "Got a 361 - see-eye version of the Chrysler hemi vee eight under there."

The old man whistled dutifully.

Trying hard not to smile, the dead man turned the key. Its thirst sated, if only temporarily, the car rattled into a semblance of life and then the engine caught and held, blowing one thick plume of smoke straight back out of the tailpipe while another burst out by the side of the offside rear wheel.

"Looks like your muffler's shot," the old man yelled above the noise of the engine.

"Yep," the dead man agreed. "Car's dying, and

there ain't nothing going to save her. But then-" He smiled and shrugged his shoulders theatrically. "-I guess we've all seen better days."

"Ain't *that* a fact," the old man said. "Don't forget, now: Forest Plains."

The dead man pulled out of the station and onto the blacktop, waving. "I won't forget," he said to he man's reflection in the rear view mirror. "Forest Plains."

(2)

When does a small town stop being small?

Maybe it's this way: towns are like people. They start off small, they grow big and then they die. One way or another.

Some die because somebody moves the highway — which is like removing the artery that feeds a human heat. The result is the heart stops.

Some die because they outgrow their strength. That's the way it happened with New York and Los Angeles, with Philadelphia and St Louis. There are plenty more.

With Forest Plains it was the first way.

One time, the blacktop took a dog's leg turn and rode straight on through Forest Plains. Only in those days it wasn't a blacktop, just a pair of wagon-wheel ruts running either side of thick grass, providing link routes for the trappers and hunters trading fish and furs at the rude log stores and warehouses along the river front some eighteen miles east. Back in those days, whisky, groceries and other staples were exchanged for wool, buffalo robes, Mexican coins and ore. But then, in 1850, Kansas City was incorporated as a town and the end of the Civil War brought the railroad along with peace.

"K.C." thrived.

The Indians — who had given the town its name; "kansas" meaning "smoky" — were replaced by the cattle ranchers, driving huge herds across the endless ranges of the West to be shipped to market. And Forest Plains was forgotten.

Forest Plains.

Even the name itself was a contradiction, a dichotomy of the bare and the clothed, the arid and the wooded.

In the country surrounding Forest Plains, the land stretched effortlessly from horizon to horizon. Around Forest Plains a man could see the future and the past... where he was going and where he had been.

And, all the while, the town lay on a deathbed of its own making, pulling in sharp breath-rattles where once it had pulled in fresh, clean air.

Crossing over Main Street between Barry Lozier's General Store and Barry's storage shack on the one side, and Griffin Stolkin's auto repair shop and the boarded-up funeral parlour on the other, West Street became East Street before getting tangled up in both directions in sugar maple and red oak, sassafras and hickory. On Main Street itself, a dusty road bordered by buildings for only three hundred seventeen yards, and which later became limestone, unstriped asphalt, striped asphalt, two-lane concrete and, finally, the divided four-lane ribbon of I-70 and its predecessor, U.S 40 — along which a dead man steered his dying automobile, looking for a turnoff that said FOREST PLAINS — the townsfolk talked about the coming of the season the way they talked about the coming of every season, their voices hushed but polite, their faces bathed in gentle but tired smiles.

Sitting on an upturned half-barrel on the boardwalk outside of the General Store, a girl stared up the road. Her name was Sara —"Like the desert," she used to tell strangers until there were no more strangers who didn't already know. Truth was Sara was like the desert in more ways than a simple contrived similarity in pronunciation. She was aloof and self-sufficient, and yet secretly lonely and dependent on the brief conversations of others.

Sara nodded to Bill McCandless and his wife, Irene as they stepped off the dusty street onto the boardwalk, intent on passing her by in silence on their way into a store. The woman ignored her but the burly man tipped his wide-brimmed hat in response.

"Hot enough for you, Mr McCandless?" Sara trilled in a come-on voice. She had watched Bill McCandless's piggy eyes trying to see down her blouse when she served him coffee and a Danish every morning, delighting in every bead of sweat that ran down that lined forehead. She turned and looked up at him, shielding her eyes from the sun's glare with one hand. With the other hand she wafted the neck of her blouse so that it popped a couple of buttons and revealed a swell of rusty-brown breast.

Oblivious, Irene McCandless pulled open the screen door and stepped into the cool darkness of Barry Lozier's store. Her husband held the door for a few seconds, smiled and nodded, then followed obediently, the door clanking behind him pushing a pleasantly cooling draught onto the boardwalk where the sun absorbed it, quickly and without mercy.

Fastening the buttons on her blouse, Sara turned back to the road and chuckled to herself. She tried to imagine Bill McCandless in the nude, his checkered shirt, with the ever present leather glasses-pouch and ball-point pens still clipped to the pocket, hanging on the back of the wicker chair in her bedroom; baggy blue work pants draped across the foot of the bed; voluminous Fruit of the Looms and two holey socks lying in a crumpled pile on her rug.

In her mind's eye, she imagined his big, white belly, filled with Coors and Miller Light, and criss-crossed with blue lines like the map of the state. And then she imagined his tiny pecker flushed out with blood, its end bruised and purple, quivering with anticipation, nosing its way out of a straggly thatch of greying pubic hair like a prairie dog checking the day from its tumbleweed home.

Lonesome Roads

She slapped her knee and shook her head, laughing, her black hair flouncing across her knees like storm clouds. When she looked up again, she saw the column of dust approaching the town.

(3)

The dead man found the turning and took a right.

He drove alongside grassed-over railroad tracks for a couple of miles before the tracks, as though bored with his company, suddenly swept away to the left and disappeared behind the trees.

He passed a wide pond that was still and mysterious, its water green and furry near the banks. A wooden sign beside it read *Darien Lake*. The sign had been uprooted and now lay at the side of the road, partially covered by the long grass. The dead man smelled a young death there, but it wasn't the one he sought.

Another mile along the road, he passed an arrowed sign showing a smiling trout waving one of its fins, and faded, red lettering that said: *Fish Camp — Tackle and Bait*. Hidden by the trees around the bend indicated by the arrow was an old shack, its boards mildewed and rotten. The split sign above gaping and disused doorway said in bold letters, *Bait and*. The rest was missing.

Eventually the trees gave out to rolling meadowland that stretched up on either side of the road, beside which wire-free telegraph poles stood in various stages of decay, leaning this way and that like good old boys with maybe one too many beers under their belts. Every now and again he saw small homesteads nestled in amongst the greenery, each sporting its own winding, dusty, single-lane track from the road. Some of these homes were accompanied by a barn or other outbuilding, while others featured old, choked-up autos rusting in the sunshine. By the time the rickety buildings of Main Street came into view down the road ahead, he had counted twenty three of them. But not a single person.

He drove into the smells of Forest Plains a little before midday, with the sun glaring down and the faint breeze blowing heat and dust and the scent of old wrongs, much stronger now, through the open window of his car.

(4)

He pulled his car up to the boardwalk in front of the general store and slid out into the light. A young Indian girl sitting on an upturned barrel watched him intently. He nodded and smiled at her. She returned the nod but not the smile.

The girl was in her early twenties, hair as black as a raven's coat and eyes of almost as deep a blue. Her face, too, was dark and brooding and the dead man noticed the early signs of a downy brown moustache on her upper lip. The additional hair suggested an impure lineage. She was maybe three or four times removed from her tribe. Sioux, he guessed; probably Lakota.

"Hey there." he said.

"Hey yourself."

He nodded to the screen door behind the girl. "This where I can get the best breakfast or lunch I ever had?"

The girl's eyes remained on the man's face.

"Call it whatever you want." she said, her words soft and couldn't-care-less. "The food's the same anyways."

"So I been told."

The girl frowned.

The man thumbed at the road he had just driven. "Fella about ten miles back, in the filling station."

Her eyes registered her understanding, though she made no other movement.

The man stood his ground. "You work here?"

"Yes, I do."

"You the cook?"

She screwed up her eyes and shook her black

tresses emphatically. "Do I look like a cook?"

The dead man chuckled the start of an apology but she cut him off.

"Nossir, I am *not* the cook: that's Mrs. Lozier. Mrs. Fay Lozier. I just do the waitressing."

"But you know what I can have, yeah?"

"Same as you can have every day of the week, every week of the year."

He smiled, hitched up his pants and took a sideways glance along the street. Down the boardwalk a couple of old men sat on uncomfortable-looking wooden chairs, watching him. He nodded to them but they didn't respond; just sat there watching him like a couple of old dogs sitting in the shade, watching humanity but not understanding it too well. The dead man turned back to face the girl. "And that is?"

She looked puzzled.

"The food."

"Steak and eggs, as many fries and pancakes as you can eat, and enough coffee to float the fleet." The words were well rehearsed.

"Sounds good."

"We ain't had no complaints." The girl leaned back against the wall, pulling the shade of the shingled roof down around her face so she could get a better look at the stranger.

He was tall, around six-two, and wore a tight-fitting, short-sleeved shirt decorated in a criss-cross pattern of inter-connecting parallel lines, and a leather vest, complete with collar and tassled, silver buttons. Down below the shirt was a thick, leather belt, worn and faded in parts, sporting an elliptical shield buckle with what looked like a bullet dent in the top right corner. The belt held up a pair of blue jeans with the usual white faded, soft-looking area just left of his zipper. She could clearly see the gentle lump beneath it. On his feet he wore a pair of brown boots, down at the heel and coming away from the sole at the left toe-cap.

"You miss anything?"

She suddenly looked up from the man's feet and met his eyes with her own. He was smiling. No, she realised, his whole *face* was smiling, creasing itself up like a catcher's mitt beneath a thick shock of greying black hair. As she watched, he ran a thick muscular hand through it to lift it from his forehead. It was brown, that face, and lined: deep brown — like the stones by the side of the railroad tracks — and deep lines, cut and worked into his skin over some... what? thirty years? She looked deeper. No, some thirty *thousand* years.

Because that's what it was: not just one man's face but the face of the entire Indian nation. It was a proud face, defiant, brave and trusting. But there was even more to it than that. Sara stared at it like it was freeze-framed on the television, drinking in every meandering track, pausing at every feature.

Sure, those traits were there, but the negative sides of them were not. Or, at least, she couldn't see them. There was no obduracy, no intransigence, no cruelty, no naiveté. It was strong without being oppressive, fair without being weak. It was...

He laughed and shook his head, rubbing his chin. There was only the faintest sign of stubble, running down from each side of his full-lipped mouth like dust.

"Huh?" she said.

"Hey, I know I must look a little road-weary but you're acting like I growed myself a third eye."

The girl rose to her feet and shook out her skirt, petulance and embarrassment colouring her cheeks like the finest rouge. "You got a name?" she asked, throwing the words over her shoulder as she pulled open the screen door.

The man nodded and smiled. "Yeah, I got a name."

She slouched back and placed her free hand on her hip, still holding the screen door wide. He could see the dim interior of the general store, could see the tables running down along side the old counter, could hear the rusty whine of electric fans holding the heat at bay. "You wanna tell me what it is?"

The smells sailed out on the fanned breeze. Steak, eggs, potatoes, coffee... guilt. And death. Old death. *Wrong* death.

When you tell a man your true name you give him a power over you, the dead man's grandfather had told him. *It was the first thing we did that was wrong.*

He looked away and stared back up the road out of town. The road he had travelled in on. The road that had brought him back to life.

He looked back at the girl, saw her questioning eyes. "Lazarus," he said at last.

She frowned. "That your first name or your last?"

"That's all of it." He shrugged. "Just Lazarus."

The girl kept on looking at him.

"How about you?"

"Sara," she said, "like the desert." And she walked inside the store.

(5)

You cannot see a smell. Not really.

But think of how they do those heat detector glasses, the ones that show you where the thermal currents are. Well, if you've got *the nose* — and there are not too many around, not any more — then you can see the smells, travelling up and down and around... coming from everywhere, going to everywhere.

For Lazarus, walking into Barry Lozier's General Store was like stepping into the tomb of some old, Egyptian king. The store itself stretched back and to either side from the door towards a bar that ran the full length across to the right and curved around to the left right in front of him.

In the recessed areas at either side of the door stood a couple of old single-bar display racks from which hung a collection of checkered shirts in a variety of sizes. The colours were different but the design was the same on all of them. Jammed between the castored feet of the racks were some old cardboard boxes, their flaps standing proud. In the boxes, Lazarus could see shorts and vests, ladies underwear and soft looking blouses, all enclosed in plastic. The bar drifted around and ran down the left of the store to a pool table. The felt was ripped and stuck over with Scotch-tape. Four balls were waiting. A cue lay across the table widthways, another stood against it. Leaning against the counter in front of the table was a large man, muscle gone to fat, slow-footed and slow-witted. He carried the look of men who have lost their way and mean to make someone else pay for it. The man, who was in the process of lighting a cigarette — Marlboro (of course) Lazarus could smell the tobacco — stood with his Zippo lighter lit, poised in the action of leaning into the flame. He was watching Lazarus.

A little way in front of him, sitting at the counter, an old man nursed a cup of coffee. He was not watching Lazarus but staring at a calendar thumb-tacked on the wall directly in front of him at the other side of the walkway behind the counter. The old man's mouth moved, fast and silent, twittering like a squirrel's, and he kept on adjusting his shoulder like his coat was slipping off.

Behind the counter right in front was Barry Lozier. Lazarus knew this because the man wore an apron with the words I'M BARRY LOZIER... WHO'RE YOU? boldly imprinted across the large pocket that bulged around his stomach. Barry Lozier was also watching Lazarus.

The girl called Sara walked briskly around the raised flap in the counter and picked up a pad of paper and a pencil. She walked back through the gap and stood beside a recessed table over to the right against the windows. For a second, the dead man couldn't understand why he hadn't been able to see into the store from out on the boardwalk but then he realised that the scene on the windows was some kind of painted mural: a town scene not unlike the real Main Street of Forest Plains, but dated around fifty years earlier. "You gonna sit down or are you gonna stand there all afternoon?"

Lazarus smiled and walked towards her.

He stepped through the smells like an explorer working his way through the fronds of a million spiders.

Here was a cheap perfume, there some aftershave and over here a waft of muscle-relaxant cream. Everywhere, the tendrils of sweat and dirt hung like a rotting curtains. As he shuffled into the booth he caught the fishy smell of the girl's private parts and the unmistakable steely odour of blood. She had her period, he realised suddenly, the thought making his cheeks redden. In the booth in front of him sat a fat man in a checkered shirt — he had his back to Lazarus — and a woman wearing RayBan sunglasses and a couple of inches of face powder.

"What'll it be?"

"I'll have the meal," he said.

"Coffee?"

He frowned and chewed his lip. "Bring me a Coke, Diet."

The girl nodded, turned around without writing anything and walked back behind the counter where she disappeared through a swing door in the wall.

At the far end of the store, further along from where Lazarus was sitting, another man appeared. Right away, Lazarus saw that this man and the one over the pool table were some kind of double act: Fred and Barney... Scooby and Shaggy. He smiled. The man caught the smile and slowed up as he approached Lazarus. Lazarus nodded. The man nodded back, frowning, then walked on past towards the pool table.

A minute later, he came back and sat on one of the revolving stools along the front of the counter. His buddy, his cigarette finally lit, sat beside him and swung around so he could stare at Lazarus.

"Where you headed?" The voice was higher

than it should have been coming out of that body, another reason for the man's disillusionment with life.

Lazarus turned to face the man. "Oh, just travelling," he said. He smiled.

The man's face remained deadly serious. Beside him, his friend slouched on the bar, his back to Lazarus.

"You?" said Lazarus.

The man's friend's back seemed to tense though he appeared not to move.

The man lifted his cigarette and took a draw, letting the smoke curl up out of his mouth. "I live here," he said. He said it strangely, Lazarus thought, without any inflection on the word 'live'.

Lazarus nodded. "Looks like a nice town," he said, still nodding.

Behind the counter, Sara appeared out of the swing door. She carried a plate of steaming food and a smaller plate piled high with pancakes. These she sat on the counter and then disappeared again.

Lazarus watched as the man with the cigarette lifted a French fry from the plate and dropped it into his mouth.

"Tastes good," the man said, chewing.

"Wayne!"

The man turned around and lifted his shoulders in a 'who, me?' gesture. "What'd I do?"

"You stole the man's food is what you did," Barry Lozier said in what sounded like an upstate New York accent. "You do it again and I'm gonna have to... to ask you to leave."

The man turned back and pulled on his cigarette. "It was just a crummy potato fry," he said to Lazarus.

"Yeah, but it was *my* crummy potato fry."

The man with his back to Lazarus seemed to twitch.

Wayne glared at him through his cigarette smoke.

Sara appeared again, this time with a tray. On the tray was a can of Diet Coke, a glass, mustard, relishes,

Lonesome Roads

ketchup, pickles, syrup and a fresh pot of coffee. She walked through the gap in the counter and, setting the tray on Lazarus's table, unloaded everything.

Wayne tapped his friend on the shoulder.

"Hey, John," — he pronounced it *Jarn*, — "know the difference between a squaw and a icebox?"

Jarn did not respond.

Wayne smiled, glancing across at Sara's back and registering Lazarus's eyes. "A icebox don't fart when you take your meat out of it."

Wayne's wheezy laugh sounded like a busted fan, high pitched and grating.

Lazarus glanced at Sara. She was ignoring the men. Lazarus decided he would, too. For now.

"Don't talk dirty, Wayne." The man had not turned his head, he just kept on looking across the bar.

Wayne pulled a face and shrugged. "Only havin' a little fun is all."

"Yeah, well," John said and let it rest.

Sara turned around and picked up the plates and carried them to the table, set them down in front of Lazarus, and then stepped back waiting for his reaction.

Lazarus leaned into the rising steam from the food. "Mmmm-*mmm*, but that smells *good*."

"Like I say, ain't had no complaints," she said, lifting a strand of black hair off her forehead.

He held his head over the food, closed his eyes and breathed it all in. *All* of it. "Know what it smells like to me?" he said.

"Like a steak?"

Lazarus nodded. "What else?"

The girl giggled, looked around at Wayne and John — the icebox crack forgotten — and frowned. "Eggs?" she said at last.

"Yes, eggs," Lazarus said. "Other things, too."

"What other things?" Wayne said.

Lazarus breathed in the food.

(6)

He breathed in Barry Lozier's General Store.
Sucked in Main Street, sucked it dry.
Drank in Forest Plains.

At first, it made him dizzy. It was like swimming in the torrent of a raging river, the water taking his head and ducking it down into the depths every few seconds. He couldn't breathe. It washed over him, buffeted him, shook him until he thought he couldn't take any more.

The girl whose name was like the desert watched the man. He was having some kind of fit. She'd heard about this kind of thing before, read about it in *The Enquirer.* He looked like he was going to up chuck right over his dinner. She stepped back against Wayne's legs and watched.

And Wayne watched.

And, next to Wayne, John watched.

And, from the other side of the counter, Barry Lozier watched.

In the adjoining booth, Barry McCandless grabbed hold of his wife Irene's arm and started to shuffle along the seat towards the aisle, pulling her with him.

Along the counter, the old man kept on staring at the calendar. A Vargas drawing of a girl in a greeny yellow dress stared back at him, pouting.

Lazarus felt sick. And hot. And cold.

The words of Chief Seattle of the Suqwamish and Duwamish rolled around his head, like a roulette ball travelling in a steadily decreasing circle as it lost its momentum. *All things are connected. Whatever befalls the earth befalls the children of the earth.*

"What the hell is wrong with him?" Wayne whispered.

Nobody answered.

Lazarus no longer heard the words around him.

As he opened fully to his gift, all extraneous noise stopped to be replaced by the sounds of the smells.

He heard the rush of the water in the river, and the keening cry of the eagles as they circled the peaks like feathered necklaces.

He heard the groan of the wagon wheels crushing the earth, and the sibilant sigh of the locomotive as it thundered along the singing rails.

He heard... many things. And each of the smell-sounds brought with it its own pain, a pain of change and of loss.

Gift! The word held a hollow ring for Lazarus. It was the only thing that he had ever possessed that he would trade without the slightest second thought.

But now, as always, he shed the last vestiges of reluctance, the final veil of refusal. As ever, exhilaration, a blur of spinning colours and sounds like photographs on which the images started to talk and move as you held them in your hand.

He embraced them then, these pasts locked in the tiny myriad spicules of scent and taste and aroma. And they ran to him like children to their father.

Pawnee. He smelled Pawnee, saw in his mind's eye the gently-graded terraces overlooking the river, smelled the sod and timber lodges. Their smell was strong, though there were also the traces of Cheyenne and Arapaho, Comanche, Kiowa and Lakota. The Lakota smell was also strong.

He smelled the campfires and the stories told around them. He smelled the expressions on the children's faces as they sat, cross-legged, their faces aglow as much with wonder as with the reflected heat of the fire.

He smelled the old tales, breathed in the brittle but strong construction of their words: scented the syntax, tales of *Maka*, the earth, and of *Maka-akan*, his spirit; tales of *Hanwi*, friend of the Lakota, whose smiling face lights the *hanhepi*... keeps *Gnaski* at bay; tales of *Ibom*, whose swirling winds destroyed many villages; and of *nagila*, the inner flame which, together with *nagi, niya* and *sicun*, binds the soul to the body.

Suddenly he was falling.

He could feel the heat from the fire, hear its crackle.

He could hear the rustle of the tepees and the swish of the horses...

He pulled back sharply and raised his hands high. "*Taku Skanskan!*" he shouted. "Lift me!"

Inside the store, the air was thick and cold. Nobody spoke, only watched.

Lazarus thumped his hands onto the table, rattling the plate of food. Then he was still again.

He was spinning upward, leaving the fires and the buffalo and the endless plains far behind him. But he was not travelling geographically, he was travelling temporally, the years spinning alongside him like a windblown dust, travelling towards Forest Plains and Barry Lozier's General Store, all of which were as yet simply great trees still yet to be felled.

He smelled the tanners and the buffalo hides.

He smelled the wooden sleepers of the railroad.

Then he smelled Texas Longhorns and splenic fever.

He smelled the sweat, a lot of sweat... the birth of Forest Plains.

The smell of the automobile.

Civilisation.

He smelled a hundred thousand people, their individual essences drifting on the time-winds like seeds. Men and women, boys and girls. He smelled their laughter and their tears, picked out their efforts with his nose, revelling in their triumphs and wallowing with them in their despairs.

He was getting closer. He could sense it.

They watched him, this strange Indian man.

They saw the sweat on his brow, saw the black hair paste down against his skull, watched his eyes dart around their sockets beneath his closed lids.

Then he smelled the scent of death. There was

a lot of death, but one death came through strongest.

It was a woman! Lazarus laughed a mighty laugh and thumped the table again. "The dead woman's here!"

Dreams.

Can you smell a dream? Lazarus could. It smelled like sarsaparilla, fizzy bubbles drifting up the passages of his nose.

It was a dream of escape, this dream among the many. Of getting out. This dream had a secondary smell, a scent of aspiration. It was a dream of the Big City, its towering spires and endless avenues stretching upwards. The images came first from picture books and then from books without any pictures. Some of the words he smelled in the woman's mind he recognised. They were names.

Whitman. Melville. Sandburg. Dickinson. Frost.

He smelled/heard her say the words, intoning them like secret karmic pledges, aural runes.

Then: more sweat.

Lazarus gagged, brought bile up into his mouth and swallowed. It tasted like battery acid.

He smelled the woman giving herself.

He smelled money.

He smelled—

"No!" He leapt to he feet, turning the table over and spilling his plate across the floor.

For what seemed like a long time, Wayne, Jarn, Sara, Bill McCandles and his wife, Irene, plus Barry Lozier — even the old timer who had been talking to the breeze and watching a girlie calendar for a sign of movement — watched the food splatter across the floor. Nobody said a word, and it fell to the proprietor to break the spell.

"Jesus Christ almighty!" Barry Lozier shouted as he ran out from behind the counter.

Wayne backed away between the stools. "What's the matter with him? He havin' a fit?"

"You okay, mister?" Sara asked softly, resting her hand on Lazarus's outstretched arm.

He opened his eyes and nodded. "I've found her," he said.

(7)

His name was not Lazarus.

Nor was he a dead man.

But, in many respects, both labels labels were appropriate, though each was a paradox of the other

For him, the country itself was a lifeless version of an earlier condition. It was not a condition which he had personally experienced but rather one which he had come across during many trips along the olfactory highways, which, to him, were as natural as the road he had ridden just hours before in his dying Dodge.

But these were highways without hard shoulders or white lines, bizarre blacktops in the ether that stretched far forward and long back, lacking directional signs or mile counters, bereft of warnings and advice. On these roads, one element was the same as any other — rain, snow, sun, wind — and nothing froze his bones, blew his hair, dampened his clothes or roasted his skin. All there was was the smell.

And the memories.

They had trooped out of Barry Lozier's General Store like an old-fashioned wagon train. The man the others knew as Lazarus led the way, his hands stretched out to either side like aircraft wings which held some secret power of divination.

Nobody spoke.

Behind Lazarus, the girl with the heart of the desert stepped lightly but with a surety that she had never felt before.

Behind her came the two men, Wayne and John, the one bearing an expression of reluctant obeisance mixed with fierce scepticism; the other carrying on his face a haunted and troubled frown.

Then came the McCandlesses, a double act, pomp and circumstance, two figures lovingly fashioned from Playdough, pudgy arms linked in something resembling an embrace, each of their small, fat faces lost in secret concerns.

Barry Lozier held open the screen door of his general store to allow the old man room to move through onto the street, while throwing his apron back into the store and shouting to his wife — the hidden cook of the greatest dinner or breakfast in the world — that he would be back later; that he didn't know how long he was going to be; and that she should close up for the afternoon. Once on the street, Barry slapped the old guy gently on the shoulder and jogged past to fall in beside Wayne and John.

The old man, now the octogenarian backmarker and resembling for all the world a bandage-less Kharis from the old *Mummy* movies, set each shaky foot onto the ground with an almost profound deliberation while balancing his tortuous gait with his spindly arms.

All around them the wind blew along the street.
The smell came with it.

(8)

He had his eyes closed for he did not need the power of sight.

He knew the street was not deserted. The wind drove dust into his face, stinging his cheeks, but he still walked on.

The woman's thread was held tight but still he had to concentrate. All around drifted the old aromas: sweet grasses smoked in pipes; coils of basswood bark steeping in drums of water; willow, oak and slippery elm; chokecherry stones and thornapples; dried squash and pumpkin seasoned with maple sugar. All the traces of an old Lakota village, long gone and buried beneath the dust of Main Street, Forest Plains. And something else. A woman.

He reached the end of the street and stopped, opening his eyes. Behind him, above the soughing howl of the early afternoon wind, the footsteps stopped.

Lazarus looked around where he was standing.

To the right stood a row of buildings — the doctor's office, Bill and Irene McCandless's house, and a window displaying bridles and saddles. Standing in the doorway beside the window, a tall man stood watching, rubbing his eyes.

To the left of Lazarus, a row of wooden fencing ran to the end of the street. It was to the fencing that Lazarus turned. "A shovel," he said. "I need a shovel."

Barry Lozier looked questioningly at Wayne and John, then ran across to the man standing in the doorway. As he reached the man, Barry was surprised to see he was crying.

"My mom..." the man said, the tears rolling down his cheeks.

"Max, what's wrong?"

"I can smell my mom, Barry. Breck shampoo. She always used Breck shampoo..." His eyes had a glassy sheen, staring over Barry Lozier's shoulders to the street beyond. But they were looking — or seeing — further than a few yards.

"Max-"

"She used to wash her hair four, maybe five times a week. Like Mary Martin in the ads in *The Post*...You know, Mary Martin from *South Pacific*?"

"I know, Max," Barry started to say, but the other man was not listening.

"She's out there."

Barry took hold of the man's arm as he started to move past him. "Max, your mom's dead." Max Saalfield turned to look at him. "She's been dead a long time, Max," Barry went on.

"But... I can *smell* her, Barry."

25

Lonesome Roads

Barry Lozier turned to the street and, against his better judgement, breathed in.

At first it was just a smell of metal, like old tin cans or auto parts. And then, like a mist, it cleared.

"Jesus Christ," Barry whispered.

He smelled his old lead soldiers and the two piece Ralston Purina truck his mother bought him from Dalton's Toystore in Kansas City, way back in 1950. Then he smelled the sugar scent of Hunt's ketchup. "Tommy?" Barry Lozier said to the wind.

Tommy Lozier, who had delighted in covering every meal placed before him with thick oodles of Ketchup, had drowned in Darien Lake in 1974. Ten years old.

"Tommy?" he asked again, though his head asked a different question: his head asked what the hell he was doing, standing beside Max Saalfield in the afternoon street, the wind blowing all around him, the pair of them calling up the dead. But then, it wasn't him or Max who was doing the calling up. It was the Indian.

Barry looked across the street and watched Lazarus. He was kneeling down beside the fence, pulling boards apart and lifting the stones from the exposed vacant lot that used to house Dan Morton's Auto Emporium. He recognised, now, the smell of Dan's one-time 'Special Buy', a deep red 1957 Chrysler Imperial hard-top that he would have given his right arm to buy. He could almost taste the wine-and-white vinyl interior and the wine-red carpeting in the trunk.

He watched Lazarus start to scrape the dirt away with his hands.

"I need a shovel, Max," Lazarus said.

(9)

It took just a little over an hour to expose the body.

(10)

"Her name was Julia."

Lazarus stood back from the hole he had dug by the side of the fence and listened to the man called John.

"She and I were going together," John went on, speaking dreamily. "We made all kinds of plans for leaving, leaving Forest Plains and heading off to the city." He stopped and stared down into the hole. "Then, one day, she just upped and left. Didn't leave no note, no forwarding address, no nothing."

Except for the checkered blue dress and the thick thatch of black hair around her wizened, grinning skull, there was little to suggest the sex of the body. It lay just a few feet below the surface, curled up like it was asleep.

"Took all her clothes, too," John went on, pointing to the crumpled mess of clothing that the Indian had pulled out on the way down to the body.

Sara moved forward and looked down. She grimaced and pulled back quickly. "When was this?"

"Fourteen years ago," John said, maintaining his matter-of-fact tone. "Used to be there was a lot of trucks went by on the spur to the Interstate. I figured she'd just gone and left me for the city."

Lazarus knelt by the hole and reached down, taking hold of the frail hand crusted with dirt. He breathed in.

Hopes.

Hopes and dreams.

He smelled determination to get out of the town... to take her man and ride the dusty blacktop to somewhere where there was no flatness. Because, the smell told him, there is no mystery to flatness. Only certainty. A certainty that nothing's coming. Nothing's going to change.

He pulled in a little deeper.

Sperm.

He smelled semen, more than one blood type.

As if on cue, John started to speak again.

"She said she was only doing it for me."

"Doing what?" Sara asked the question softly.

"She-."

"She was a hooker," Wayne said. "I'm sorry, John."

John appeared to take no offence. "She said she was doing it so's we could get ourselves a little extra money. Looks like she pulled one trick too many."

As John continued to speak, Lazarus brushed the dirt away from the woman's stomach and exposed the slit in her dress. There was a long gash that stretched all the way across from her stomach to her right side, the side she was lying on.

"It's strange, you know?" John went on. "I want to feel sad... to cry or somethin'. But, in a way, I feel kind of relieved. I mean-"

Lazarus lifted the woman's right hand up and pulled it free of her body. It was clenched tight.

"-she didn't leave me-"

It was holding something.

"-after all."

Lazarus pulled the fingers apart, cringing at the dusty crack as they snapped and separated open.

"What is it?" Sara said.

"You find something?" said Barry Lozier.

"Bill-" Irene McCandless hissed.

Bill McCandless breathed in loudly. "Oh my-"

Lazarus turned the object over in the palm of his hand. It was metal. A string tie clasp. He dusted it and turned it around so that he could read what was written on it.

"Bill. *Bill!*" Wayne gasped.

Bill McCandless started forward. "That's my-" He stopped.

The clasp featured a name scrolled in a lariat. Bill.

"You killed her?" The words were colder than an Arctic wind, and the face that said them — his face looked whiter than snow.

Everything else happened fast.

Bill McCandless stood transfixed, shaking his head. "I nev-"

John leapt across and grabbed the older man by his neck, pushing him to the ground.

Irene McCandless threw her RayBan glasses to the side and tried to pull her husband's assailant back but it was no use.

"John, I nev-" The punch landed in Bill's mouth and split his upper denture. Almost immediately, a second punch broke his nose.

Barry Lozier threw himself across the two men and wrapped his arms around John.

Irene McCandless shuffled across on her knees to hold her husband's head. He wasn't moving. "Bill! Bill?" She shook his shoulders.

Behind her, John worked his way free of Barry Lozier and reached across for the shovel.

"*Bill!*" Irene shouted.

John lifted the shovel.

Lazarus watched.

"John for crissakes..." Wayne snapped.

"*He* didn't kill her!" Irene McCandless screamed. "*I* did."

Lazarus caught the shovel.

The wind whispered, pulled back and regrouped.

(11)

The woman sat on the ground, cradling her husband's head on her lap, rocking gently to and fro.

"I knew he'd been seeing her," she started. "Any woman knows when her man's cheating on her. But I didn't have no evidence." She straightened her hair. "Somehow, that made it okay, you know?" She looked around at the faces for confirmation and for sympathy. She didn't find any.

"Then, this one night, he came home and went to bed," she went on. "Bill sleeps like a bear in hibernation. When he closes his eyes, there's nothing gonna wake him up.

"Anyways, I went over to his clothes and checked them over — you know, for lipstick, rouge... that kind of thing?"

She had addresses this last question to Sara. Sara nodded and looked away.

"Well, I couldn't find anything.

"So, I was going back over to the bed and I caught sight of his tie-clasp — it'd fallen on the floor over by the dresser. I bent over to pick it up... and I smelled it." She nodded to the body. "*Her*. I could smell that scent she used to wear, could smell it all over my husband's tie clasp."

"Jesus," Wayne said.

"*Jesus* is right," Irene agreed. She shrugged and shook her head. "What can I tell you? I went mad, I guess. I went right over and confronted her with the clasp. She took it from me, held it in front of me. Then she told me it didn't mean nothing." She looked at the other faces again. "I couldn't take that. Not from her. '*It doesn't mean nothing,*' she says to me.

"It was then I realised I'd taken the knife."

Bill McCandles started to move. He groaned but didn't open his eyes.

"Shhh," his wife whispered, stroking his forehead. She sighed and continued her story.

"Anyways, when it was done, I carried her down to this lot, dug the hole and rolled her in. Then I went back and took all her clothes, threw them in after her." She shook her head again and turned around, a half-smile tugging at her mouth. "It's surprising what you can do when you have a min-"

If anything, the hole appeared above Irene McCandless's left eye a split second before the sound of the gun. She was dead before she fell back against the ground, her husband's head still resting on her lap.

(12)

His name was Joe, Joe Yenne.

His wife had died giving birth to their daughter, an only child who lived four hours before deciding she'd rather stay with her mother.

The years following Maggie Yenne's death had been empty years, lacking both motivation and companionship.

Then the girl had come to Forest Plains.

Her name was Julia, and she used to treat Joe Yenne like he was somebody. She would talk to him when she served him coffee, telling him about what it was like in the Big City... even though, as she freely admitted, she had never been. And she would quote things to him, lines of poetry, words that spoke about Big Cities everywhere.

She quoted from Robert Frost and Ezra Pound.

She quoted from Emily Dickinson and T.S.Eliot. From Carl Sandburg and Hart Crane.

Then they would laugh together, sharing secrets that only those people completely comfortable with each other could truly share. And the only thing that came between them was forty years, give or take a few months.

He told her he liked words, never having been much of a reader himself. And he made her a proposition.

He knew all about her dream to fly away to the Big City.

He knew all about John, too. He'd seen the way they looked at each other at Barry Lozier's General Store.

So he told her he would pay to have her read to him, read him poetry.

At first she had laughed. But he was serious, he told her.

Then she had laughed again, even as she read him *Oklahoma* by Ernest Hemingway. She chose that poem,

31

she told him, because it summed up everything she wanted to escape from:

The prairies are long,
The moon rises
Ponies
Drag at their pickets
The grass has gone brown in the summer --
(or is it the hay crop failing)

He had read and reread the poem from the book she had loaned him, committing that stanza to memory.

And sometime later, months later, she had revisited the poem with him following an unpleasant incident with a truck driver. Barry Lozier had thrown the guy out — even before he had even a chance to pay for his meal — but not before he'd made a few cracks, mean cracks.

Oh, the fella hadn't meant anything by them, but they'd hurt Julia just the same.

"*Know what the difference is between a squaw and a proctologist?*" the man had asked her. "*A proctologist only has to look at one arsehole at a time.*"

And:

"*What does a waitress say after sex? 'Gee, are all you fellas on the same team?'!*"

She had told him the Indian's day in this country was finished and that Hemingway had prophesied it in Oklahoma.

All of the Indians are dead.
(A good Indian is a dead Indian)

"That's us, Joe," she said to him, her eyes glistening. "Dead people... dead men, dead women."

As he told this part of the story to the others, standing around her grave, a single tear popped from each of his eyes and ran down to the sides of his chin. He made no effort to stop them and went on with his story.

One day, she didn't show up for work.

The next day was the same.

And the next.

And Joe Yenne was alone once more. With nothing to hold his interest during the long wait except the Vargas girls on Barry Lozier's calendar.

(13)

Lazarus was the first to speak.

"Put the gun away," he said. "Take it home, and put it away."

"Hey, now wait a min-"

Lazarus turned to Barry Lozier and shook his head.

"Shhh," he said. He turned back to the old man. "Joe Yenne, I have something for you."

The old man nodded.

"It is a gift. The gift of knowledge."

He nodded again.

"But like all knowledge," Lazarus said, "its strength lies in its secrecy. Knowledge shared is power weakened. It is a mistake my people began to make and then saw their mistake. Better to die strong than to live weak. Do you understand?"

Another nod.

"Listen then." Lazarus leaned foreard and whispered in the old man's ear. This close, Lazarus could smell the old man's pancreatic cancer stronger than ever. It shifted and growled like the mountain cat, turned and hissed like the cyclone.

Lazarus finished speaking and stepped back. He said, "Do you *really* understand?"

Joe Yenne smiled. "Yes, I understand."

"Then you must go."

The old man turned around, the gun still hanging limply from his hand, and walked back the way they had come.

"We'll have to tell the sheriff," Barry Lozier said.

"Of course," said Lazarus.

Barry turned to look at the other man, surprised.

"They'll go out to get him."

"Mm hmm," he said. "But he won't be there."

"Where'll he go? He's just an old man."

"Oh, he's not too old for the kind of travelling *he* must do... but he's going too far for you to follow," came the answer. "For some time, anyways."

(14)

"What did you say to him?" Sara asked as they watched John and Wayne carry Irene McCandless's body along the street.

Lazarus cocked his head on to one side and frowned.

"Okay, okay, I know — mind my own business." She smiled and shrugged. "Will he—" She nodded to Bill McCandless, who was sitting against the fence staring along Main Street to the flatlands beyond, the opposite direction to that now being travelled by his late wife. "-be okay?"

"He'll be as okay as he will ever be" Lazarus answered, "or as he has ever been."

It wasn't the kind of answer Sara wanted, but it was the only one she knew she was going to get.

Lazarus walked across to the hole, knelt beside it and reached down.

"What are you doing now?" Barry Lozier asked, the sound of his exasperation sounding clearly in his voice.

"I'm turning her around," Lazarus said.

"Turning her *around?*"

"*In spite of all the learned have said,*
I still my opinion keep;
The posture, that we give the dead,
Points out the soul's eternal sleep."

He turned around and looked up at the girl and the man watching him.

"A poem: it figures," Barry Lozier said, and he walked off to get the shovel.

As Lazarus got to his feet and dusted off his hands Sara said, "I ain't never read much poetry. Is it... is it all like that? Pretty, I mean."

"Some of it is, some isn't. It's like everything else, means different things to different people. Like the desert," he added, smiling at her.

Sara returned the smile and glanced away. When she looked back, Lazarus had turned around and was starting to walk back along the street to where a dusty Dodge sat beside an empty general store. "Was it yours?" she called after him. "The poem?"

He turned back and shook his head. "No. It is called *The Indian Burying Ground*, by Philip Freneau."

Sara nodded. "*The Indian Burying Ground*. I guess she'd like that."

He twirled his car keys around on his finger, threw his head back and breathed in through his nose. Behind him, Barry Lozier was shovelling dirt into the hole. When Lazarus lowered his head again, he was smiling. "She does," he said.

Sara watched him all the way back to his car, then watched the car as it, too disappeared. Then all that was left was the magic light of late afternoon, the faint, tinkling echo of the dead man's car keys and the sweet smell of resolution.

Lonesome Roads

Standby

> The seed you sow does not come to life
> unless it has first died.
> *1 Corinthians, 15*

> Something was dead in each of us,
> And what was dead was Hope.
> Oscar Wilde,
> *'The Ballad of Reading Gaol'*

(1)

John didn't see the man until he was almost past the alley. Up ahead, the lights at the intersection had just turned to red.

Even then, he only caught sight of the figure — just a bum shambling out of the dark shadowy recess between the bricked walls, tired of talking to the demons in his brown paper bag — because he was staring at his passenger, trying for one more time to see even the faintest glimmer of recognition, of *any* expression at all, on her face.

Traffic was blocked heading out to Montauk because of roadworks, stop-starting in a steady stream, a lot of low-gear work which only bothered those drivers with manual transmissions. In the other direction it was flowing fast and smooth.

All around him, John could sense the mounting frustration. It was a late October afternoon, and folks were anxious to get away from where they didn't want to be any more and safe where they *did* want to be, motivated by the encroaching darkness.

When the car behind honked, John turned back to the road and edged forward the few yards that had opened up while his attention had been distracted, closing up on the fender and the JESUS SAVES sticker on the rusting Buick in front. Then the line moved forward again, just a few more yards, and came to a stop.

Lonesome Roads

More horns blared behind him.

John turned to wave to the guy in the car behind him... to maybe slip him the bird

What can I do, asshole!

but when he shuffled full around he saw that the man behind him was himself turned looking at the sidewalk he had just passed. Something was happening a few cars down the line but John couldn't make out what it was because of a truck two cars back. He glanced across at the side mirror.

It was the bum. He was on the sidewalk now, shambling along in the direction of the traffic, moving slow. The guy really looked the part: pants legs too short by around a foot, jacket three or four sizes too small, and no shirt — at least, none that John could see. And he was carrying... what was that? an umbrella? That was okay — it was raining, although not hard — but he hadn't even bothered to open it up.

And whoever heard of a bum carrying an umbrella?

That's when John noticed that the bum looked like the Solomon Grundy character out of the old Batman comicbooks.

The honking was coming from the cars alongside the bum, more cars adding to the noise as he moved forward. Then, when the bum was about five maybe six cars away, John saw that the umbrella wasn't an umbrella at all: it was a piece of metal bar with a base. Some of the drivers had got out of their cars — one of them was reaching a hand out to the bum. The bum turned around and swung the bar down, swung it down again. As the driver went down on the ground, the bum bent down after him.

John saw the bar-and-base come into view and then disappear again, three maybe four times, wielded one-handed no less — that was one strong hobo!

Out on the street people were shouting.

The bum stood up again, swaying a little, like he'd been drinking.

Two steps away from where the bum had surely turned the driver's head to mulch, another driver was backing away along the sidewalk. He was holding a square sign in his hands, a sign with writing on it — John could make out the words: NO WAITING... the top part of a road sign; and John had a good idea what had happened to the bottom.

The bum turned around, swinging his makeshift weapon at a man who had stepped out of a store alongside him, sending him flying backwards against and through the store window.

John was suddenly aware of someone watching him. He shifted his gaze and saw his passenger staring at the side of his head. She was... frowning? "Is... is that him?" he asked her. "Is that the man who came to the house?"

There was no answer.

He turned back. The bum was still moving, dragging the long bar-and-base contraption along the sides of the stationary traffic — the resulting damage to paintwork undoubtedly the cause of all the honking earlier. But now the drivers were not doing anything. John guessed they were probably busy making sure their doors were locked.

A woman in a high-axeled Jeep two cars back had abandoned her vehicle and was running across the road. John glanced across at the mirror beside him and saw the woman reach the sidewalk. There were people there, all of them just standing, watching. The woman was saying something to them, pointing to the bum.

John looked back at the mirror on the passenger side.

The bum seemed to look up the line and John caught his face in the mirror — it was as though he was looking right at him. Then he strode off the sidewalk somewhere behind the truck and out of sight.

"Jesus Christ, what-" John's words trailed off.

Up ahead, the lights had changed again but John's line didn't move. The traffic coming in the other direction, however — heading for the Hamptons and all points

Lonesome Roads

south-west — didn't have any such restrictions.

Faced with what appeared to be an open road, the first car through, an Eldorado, was just a little too fast off the mark and didn't see the bum stepping out in front of the truck. The driver slammed on his brakes when he was just past John's Dodge but it was too late. John watched the whole thing in his side mirror, silently marveling at the balletic grace as the Eldorado picked the man up on its hood, carried him the length of three vehicles, and stopped. The bum rolled off the hood onto the road.

John thought he heard something like a whimper from his passenger.

"It's okay," he told her. "Whoever he was, he's down now."

He opened the door and got partway out.

As he turned to face the line of traffic behind him, John's eyes locked with those of the bum — he was up off the ground looking none the worse for being tossed into the air. He was pounding the bar-and-base combination on the Eldorado's hood.

John drew in breath.

It *was* Solomon Grundy... the same washed-out white face, the same frizz of unkempt hair, the same muscles. The man finished smashing the hood of the car that had knocked him down and shambled around it.

Heading straight for John.

John got back into the car.

He looked at the woman beside him. Her eyes were still vacant, like colored marbles dropped into a mannequin's sockets, but the skin around them was creased. Was that fear?

"It's *not* okay, is it?" he asked. No answer.

"He's coming after *us*, isn't he?" Still nothing. "It was nothing to do with the house... not a robbery. It's *us* he wants."

He slipped off the handbrake and started turning the wheel hard down to the left, easing the Dodge out into the oncoming lane.

A delivery truck jumped the lights and saw what he was doing; the driver leaned on the horn and swerved around the Dodge's nose.

"Yeah, *and* you!" John shouted, pulling hard down on the wheel.

There were more horns behind him. More shouts. But no more traffic coming. John eased fully out of the line and into the other lane.

A small, low-slung continental job made a right out of Sycamore Street and pulled up right in front of John. The driver, a young guy, was mouthing at John, telling him to back the fuck up and get in his own lane.

John checked his rear-view: the bum was now out in the open road, about twenty yards back and closing, brandishing the bar-and-base like Conan the Barbarian... not moving very fast but moving fast enough. He would reach John's Dodge in just a few more seconds.

In the continental job, the young woman passenger was leaning across to look around John, pointing, telling her boyfriend to quit worrying about the guy in the Dodge because here came the Incredible Hulk

no it isn't... it's Solomon Grundy

looking pissed and twirling a hundred-pound road sign like it was a parade-leader's baton.

John eased the Dodge forward until it tapped the continental's fender, then he pumped the gas and started edging the two cars forward.

The driver in the other car looked like he was going to bust a few arteries, leaning on his horn while he stuck his head out of the window — "What the hell you doing, you crazy-"

A flatbed pickup traveling across the end of the road hit the rear wing of the continental and John missed the end of the man's speech... but he could guess what it would have been. The continental swung backwards fully out into the flow of traffic on the crossway, pinned against the light standard by the pick-up.

An old Volkswagen that was more rust than paint hammered a musical horn, swerved to avoid hitting the rear of the pick-up and ran hood-to-hood with something coming in the other direction. John couldn't make out what it was but he heard the dull crunch and saw the VW driver go forward in his seat and partway through the windshield.

Even as John stamped on the gas, there was a thud on the back of the Dodge and the sound of breaking glass. He jumped forward — allowing himself a quick glance in the rear-view to see Solomon Grundy, eyes wide as saucepan lids, pulling the road sign bar from the back window — clipped the edge of the continental's front fender (which then screeched along the Dodge's front wing), steered around the rear of the pickup and, in the adjoining lane, the back of the VW, and into the road at the other side.

As he headed towards Montauk — the sign up ahead said

next stop, The Twilight Zone

11 Miles and the Point was probably another seven or eight — people were running past him to the smashed vehicles, waving their arms

Hey come on, there's been a smash-up... maybe we'll see some bodies!

and pointing. Someone's horn was full on — John thought it might be the guy in the VW, lying half out of the car and spread-eagled on his hood (which was the VW's trunk) with his crotch resting on the steering wheel horn-press — and there were lots of shouts mingled with music playing from car radios, a litany of solitary horn-blasts and, somewhere far off but getting nearer, a siren, *wee waw*-ing like a vulture to a massacre.

"Not long now," John told his passenger. Then, more to himself, he said, "How did he know where we *were*? What does he *want*?"

She didn't say anything.

As the sky outside grew darker, John hoped things were going to turn out okay.

* * *

(2)

John Pederson was no stranger to hope. But, although he had been doing a lot of hoping, he had been getting very little payback.

He had hoped, for instance, that the small lump Helen had found in her left breast one evening in May, just six months earlier, was merely benign fibrous tissue or maybe blocked ducts that would, in the words of the doctor who saw them at the start of what turned out to be Helen's prolonged death sentence, 'resolve spontaneously'. Indeed, when he had learned that the lump — hardly a lump at all: more like a slight undulation — had not been there the previous week when Helen had performed her regular check the doctor suggested she go away and come back the following week if the lump had not disappeared.

John and Helen went through a lot of hope that week. And all to no avail. The slight undulation was still there and it was maybe even a little bigger.

On the second visit the doctor booked her into the hospital in Bridgehampton for an excision biopsy.

When John asked if that was it, if that course of action would solve the problem, the doctor was noticeably cautious in his response. Not necessarily, was the answer. It would merely enable the medical team to see if the undulation was benign or malignant.

More hope. John had begun to feel that he may not have enough. He had wished, on one long night, with the darkness outside the house seeming to push at the windows so it could swirl in and engulf him, that there was a drug store that sold hope in bottles and tubs. Like one of the old traveling elixir sellers, with remedies available for different things: the HERE'S HOPING I WIN THE LOTTERY lotion, maybe, or the HERE'S HOPING I GET A DATE WITH BARBARA balm... and, of course, the HERE'S HOPING MY WIFE DOESN'T HAVE CANCER cream, '... to be applied liberally to the affected area'.

43

But there were no such secret supplies and John's home-grown hope proved to be insufficient for the job in hand. The undulation was malignant.

Two courses of action now presented themselves, the doctor explained. His tone was decidedly more serious.

Helen could have a lumpectomy, a curiously backwoods-sounding name for an operation which involved the removal of only the undulation and a small amount of surrounding tissue. Or they could go for the simple mastectomy.

At the time, both John and Helen thought that 'simple' was merely a word that had become attached to *any* mastectomy — a means of emphasizing not only the high incidence of the operation but also, they hoped (that word again!), the high success rate.

But, although they would never have admitted it, neither of them wanted to ask any question which might carry an answer they didn't want to hear.

Helen asked which operation the doctor suggested and she smiled, patting her husband's hand, when the man cleared his throat and recommended the simple mastectomy, emphasizing that word 'simple' again. "Better safe than sorry," he said before turning away and scanning the papers on his desk.

In early July, Helen went back to Bridgehampton and had the tissue of her left breast removed as well as the axillary nodes in her left armpit. This was not the 'simple' mastectomy: this was the full enchilada.

The surgeon had felt that, although there was no clear evidence of cancer cells in the lymph nodes of the axilla, the deterioration and spread of the disease in the breast tissue itself called for a cautionary extension of the operation. The additional work was explained away — again — as simply a case of better safe than sorry. John and Helen bought into that in a big way, neither of them commenting on the repeated use of that phrase. If anything, they felt even more hopeful than if Helen had just had the 'simple' variant.

Certainly the after-effects were not as bad as either she or John had feared, with the breast re-built using a silicone implant that, aside from the temporary discoloration of the extensively bruised flesh and a difficulty in moving her left arm, made it difficult to tell the difference from the right breast. As soon as she was recovered from the operation Helen started a series of radiotherapy sessions to zap any residual spread and a course of chemotherapy, a cocktail of cytotoxic drugs — primarily tomoxifen — to clear up anything that
better safe than sorry
managed to escape the radiotherapy.

Just one week after the operation, Helen was called into Bridgehampton for a magnetic resonance imaging, a device which didn't use X rays but which, by means of a magnetic field, enabled the doctors to see all of the soft tissue organs and to look for 'hot spots'.

John didn't much care for the phrase 'hot spots', but the results looked okay.

There followed much hand-shaking and dewy-eyed laughter from John, the saliva stringing in his mouth every time he opened it not knowing whether to laugh or cry.

Two weeks later, Helen complained of back pains. John told her she'd been spending too much time in the yard, moving plants around from the rectangular bed of soil next to the fence to the haphazard spread of the rockery. Hot baths, massages and much nervous laughter followed over the ensuing days, during which time, every now and again, John would ask his wife if it felt any better. On each of these occasions, Helen cast her eyes skyward, frowning, trying to isolate the discomfort within herself and measure it, but each time she shook her head, her heart almost breaking because she could not reassure her husband.

But, she told him, she was sure it would improve soon.

It didn't improve.

Helen went to see the doctor again, torn between telling all and trying to dismiss the problem even as she was explaining its symptoms.

The doctor listened, twirling a pencil around in his hand.

The following day, Helen and John returned to Bridgehampton for another ride on the magnetic resonance imager.

Right from the start Helen didn't much care for the somewhat official reception they were given, which was virtually devoid of smiles and pleasantries. She figured 'safe' time was over: now it was time for 'sorry'.

After Helen had got dressed, a stern-faced intern asked them both to come into his office. Helen held onto John's hand, squeezing it only slightly when the news came.

The disease had spread to Helen's bones and there was a tumor the size of a nickel — "... almost a quarter, but not quite," the intern said — on her brain. Staring wide-eyed as he listened, John fought to dispel the image of the doctors measuring the brain tumor in the back room while he and his wife had been waiting nervously in the corridor.

A nickel... I say it's a nickel.
Uh uh, more like a quarter.
How's about we go for 15 cents?
Done! Say, you going for a beer tonight...?

John wanted to know what happened now.

"It doesn't look good," the intern said, holding his eyes steadily on Helen's like he was trying to get the message across to her without using words. Helen knew what the words were: 'terminal' and a phrase denoting a span of time. The span of time, when it came, was three months. Possibly four, but that, he felt 'duty bound' to point out, was unlikely.

John had felt a sudden breathlessness at that and Helen squeezed his hand tighter, said something to the intern that John didn't quite catch. All John could hear

was the word 'unlikely'.
You think it'll rain today?
Unlikely.
Or how about:
You think maybe Springsteen'll ever reform the E Street Band?
Very *unlikely.*
And best of all:
You think maybe Helen Pederson'll make it to Thanksgiving before she turns to plant-food?
Heh... let's put it this way: buy a smaller turkey.

When John tuned back into the conversation, the intern was booking Helen a course of pain killers and a steroid — dexa-something-or-other — to reduce the swelling in the brain.

It seemed like no time at all from that fateful meeting — when John's senses were suddenly so attuned to everything in the world — to the afternoon in the side ward at Bridgehampton (euphemistically referred to as Death Row in a conversation that John happened to overhear between two orderlies) when the senior doctor suggested that they turn off the equipment.

It was October 8. She hadn't even made it to Columbus Day.

Helen was 46 years old. If Life could be said to be a big meal in your favorite restaurant, with the octogenarian dotage of forgetfulness and constantly damp Fruit of the Looms being equated with a strong coffee and a glass of port, Helen was only part-way through a plate of meatloaf, sweet potatoes, and all the vegetables and gravy that would fit.

They had stopped the steroid two days earlier, when Helen had slipped into a deep sleep that she would never wake up from, her grip on John's hand as tight as it had ever been... as though she were intent on taking him with her. He was sure that even this last act was selfless, brought about by a reluctance in his wife to leave him fending for himself as opposed to a growing panic at her imminent departure.

At that time, Helen weighed just 71 pounds.

Watching the nurses wander around the bed detaching apparatus — a syringe driver attached to a canula; a needle inserted into Helen's abdominal wall; a battery-operated pump which delivered a continuous supply of morphine... all of it had been explained to them both when she had been admitted — John couldn't help but marvel at the mental stamina required to do this work.

They left him alone with her for most of the time after that, coming back to check her 'progress'. John talked to her all the time, watching her face, searching for the slightest twitch of a muscle so that he could push a bell and see them rush into the room like they always did on *ER* or *St. Elsewhere,* one of the impossibly handsome George Clooney types shouting in amazement that it was a miracle.

But it didn't happen.

We're all outta miracles today, son... whyn't you come back and give us a try tomorrow...

With each slight rise of his wife's chest, John held his own breath waiting for Helen's next, undecided as to whether he was hoping for another or praying that she could rest now.

In those final hours, John replayed all the moments of the past few weeks... seeing Helen clearing out her wardrobes and drawers and checking through papers (which she had stacked neatly, attaching different-colored *Post-It* stickers explaining what they were), sometimes catching sad eyes with his, just for a second or two before she looked away, a sad smile playing on the corners of her mouth.

It was then, with darkness falling outside, that John Pederson promised his wife that he was not going to let this

a little thing like a swelling brain and crumbling bones

keep them apart. He promised her the thing that he had been thinking about over what seemed like hundreds of late night / early morning sessions sitting in the chair in their bedroom, watching his wife toss and turn in her sleep, wondering what she was dreaming about... thinking she was probably dreaming of leaving him. About *having* to leave him. 'The Drinker's hour' was what Tom Wolfe called it in *The Bonfire Of The Vanities*; that time in the middle of the night when a sense of pure dread grips your stomach in a vice and pulls you out of sleep, the breath catching in your throat... and each time, he would turn slowly, just his head, keeping his body rigid, feeling with his foot to see if his wife's leg was still warm... listening with his very soul to see if she was still breathing. And after that, with a return to sleep proving elusive, he would sit, the curtains blowing beside him in the breeze of another day starting up, thinking impossible thoughts.

But now the impossible thoughts would be made possible.

This he promised to his wife and himself, and to all the capricious gods and deities who saw fit to make airliners crash and have guys walk into fast food joints carrying automatic weapons.

"I *will* find a way," he told her quietly, whispering it to the side of her face as he watched her chest rise, more slowly now, more time between each gentle inhalation, a soft juddering in her cheeks and the faintest whistling sound from her throat. Death would not keep them apart. Not ever.

He told her he would bring her back.

And even as he said the words, Helen's chest lay still.

He waited, watching, his eyes straining, waited for another movement. And as the seconds piled up and that extra movement didn't come he suddenly realized that, selfish or not, he needed her to breathe again, just one more time... just one more infinitesimal movement, no

Lonesome Roads

matter that she was in a coma and no matter that the tumor on her brain was already starting to push out the left side of her head, where no luxurious hair grew any more... only intermittent tufts of stringy tonsorial crabgrass.

He laid his head on the part of the bedsheet that he knew covered the soft part of her upper thigh and felt the tears come and the bile start in his throat. And he told her again and again, was still telling her — though his voice had grown hoarse — when the doctor came in and placed a hand gently on his shoulder.

"I *will* bring you back, I promise..."

* * *

(3)

All around was the sound of chaos: shouting voices — some in pain and some in anger — car horns and sirens.

The big man stood his ground in the street watching the car disappearing across the wreckage-littered crossway, impassively watching its taillights in the gathering darkness. He still held the bar-and-base in his right hand. In his left, he held the crumpled shirt-front of a man whose head, arms and legs hung down to the ground like an old stuffed toy whose insides had grown limp.

All around the big man people were pointing and shouting at him, moving warily from side to side across the street on the sidewalk, pacing like caged animals. He ignored them and moved his head to one side, straining to make sense of the cacophony of sound. That was when he saw the stardust trailing out, high above him in the night air.

He had forgotten about it... forgotten how it had been the stardust and its thin residue that had led him to his quarry.

He closed his eyes and breathed in deeply. The smell of the dust made him want to gag. It brought with it images of where he had been for so long — the endless sea of soul-faces, jammed end-to-end for as far as he could imagine, most of them only passing time before moving on and leaving him and others like him, still jammed end-to-end, without rest or respite, without sleep or sustenance, without noise or communication.

There had been nobody to talk to and no means to talk to them. No mouth to speak with or to breathe; no eyelids to bring down for merciful darkness; no arms or legs to stretch. There had been only *them* and *the place*, their awareness of it and each other.

He would not go back.

Could not go back.

The dust would help him. It stretched over his head and — as he turned to look — behind him, though the old dust was now dissipating... a small-scale Milky Way, twinkling and shimmering and beginning to fade, 'falling' upwards.

But up ahead, where the car had disappeared, the trail was thick and vibrant and fresh. He bent his body backwards, looked up above himself and saw the tell-tale trail of stardust stretching from his own head, twisting high into the air... tiny twinkling particles of fairy dust, swirling and dancing.

He dropped the man's broken body to the ground and turned around. There was a car alongside him. He moved towards it lifting the bar-and-base. The man behind the wheel shuffled across the passenger seat and almost fell onto the street. The big man lifted his hand awkwardly and tried the door. It was locked. He pulled back and smashed the window on the driver's side, reached in and opened the door. It had been a long time since he had driven a car. He dropped the bar to the pavement and slid behind the steering wheel.

Minutes later — when he had figured out that this thing had no clutch — he was on his way, jerking and jumping, following the trail of fairy dust drifting up through the evening gloom, the dust from his own body wafting up inside the car and settling against the material-covered roof like fire-ash.

Lonesome Roads

* * *

(4)

Between leaving the hospital — walking stiltedly out in the cool air of an early autumn Bridgehampton evening, hardly taking anything in... just moving one foot in front of the other like one of the flesh-eating zombies in the George Romero movies — and now, driving through the October night to Montauk Point for the second time, John Pederson's life had been a strange and confusing helter skelter of dimly-remembered conversations, snippets of dialogue which John replayed from time to time, hearing them afresh in his head, echoing like old radio shows, the words seeming alien... as though he had not originally been a part of them.

He looked across at his wife and saw her staring waxenly straight ahead out of the windshield, apparently watching the wiper-blades move side to side against the constant drizzle although the past few days seemed to suggest that she didn't really see anything at all.

He was now through Montauk.

Turning his attention back to the road — MONTAUK POINT 4 MILES — he replayed the sequence of events that had led him to this.

Even by the time he had buried his wife, with the early fall leaves already turning a burnished red and gold on the trees in Amagansett Cemetery and the smell and sound of the Atlantic barely a mile away providing a sense of cosmic continuance, John Pederson had not exhausted his reserve of hope. But it had suddenly seemed fruitless, as though he were living in the pages of paperback novel rather than in the real world.

And for a while, the desperate promise he had made to Helen had got put to the back of the stove while he tried to get on with his life.

But getting on with his life proved increasingly difficult as the days stacked up after the funeral. The house itself was the main problem: everywhere he looked he saw traces of Helen, even though he had gone to great pains to remove many of the things that might remind him of her. That was the paradox: even the *absence* of Helen's bits and pieces served as a reminder.

Long walks away from the house didn't help. While he was out, he would find a public telephone booth, and, with a pile of quarters (it started out with just one) he would repeatedly phone the apartment just to hear

Hi, you've reached John and Helen: we're not in right now or can't get to the phone... but leave us a message and we'll get back to you. Here comes the beep...

Helen's voice on the answering machine. He could not bring himself to erase that message.

On getting back home, he would stand out on the street or sit cross-legged on the hood of the old Dodge staring at the house — at the windows that Helen had looked out of — and wonder what might happen if he closed his eyes and concentrated real hard... whether that might just bring Helen back to him... if only for a little while. If only for one night.

He tried it. Nothing happened.

But it brought the old saucepan of promise that he'd taken off the heat back onto a front burner. And as the days drifted by, he turned the power up to maximum.

He would try other things, he decided: nothing too radical, but just things that, even if they didn't actually bring Helen back into his life, would somehow heal the wound.

But nothing is that simple and the intensity of his attempts — prayers, mantras (*Please let Helen come back to me was one*) repeated over and over in the dark and moody silence of the house, touching wood three times... nothing worked and each time the realization hit him, John sank more and more into despair.

Who can say when a healthy mind goes bad?

It's like leaving a piece of fruit in the bowl and trying to see the point where it begins to rot. One minute, it looks fine and the next it's all wizened and showing patches of mold.

If one had to say when this happened to John Pederson's mind, one might hazard a guess at one of Tom Wolfe's so-called drinker's hours, when, even though he was sleeping (albeit fitfully), fetally curled up around his wife's nightdress, the irrationality of Dreamland seeped through the wafer-thin membrane tissue that usually held it at bay and mingled with John's everyday thoughts.

*When*ever or *why*ever or even *how*ever it happened, it did happen. And things were always going to get worse from there.

In this new and slightly off-kilter world-view, nothing was impossible. And so, while he accepted the failure of his very basic early ideas, John's thoughts turned to more elaborate schemes and processes to bring his wife back to him. There had to be something, but the question was where to find it.

Books, was the answer. Books, books and more books.

And that, in reality, was how it *really* started.

Some of them John found he already had, tucked away on shelves around the house, picked up over the years at garage sales or rescued from rain-lashed cardboard boxes in front of the old bookstores he and Helen always seemed to be able to find no matter where they were heading. Sometimes coverless, sometimes containing old inscriptions — *To Henry, Christmas 1944, with all my love, Carol*, said one — these invariably dog-eared tomes were mostly paperback and generally of the new age school of mystical and magical realism... shlocky *Condoms Of The Gods*-kind of stuff. But while most of them contained hints and pointers to the information he sought, none actually delivered the goods.

A chapter entitled 'Death and the Reintegration of the Group' in a badly creased Doubleday Anchor edition of Bronislaw Malinowski's *Magic, Science and Religion* provided a little early relief inasmuch that it made John feel like he was one of many — *Misery loves company*, he thought. The craving for loved ones after they had 'passed over' transcended normal grief, the piece suggested, and this seemed to endorse what John had in mind.

Geoffrey Ashe's *The Ancient Wisdom* and Stan Gooch's *Guardians of the Ancient Wisdom* were interesting but strangely insubstantial for what John was looking for, while Frank Gaynor's *Dictionary of Mysticism* and the Hermetic Museum's lavishly-illustrated *Alchemy & Mysticism* were a little too 'Carlos Casteneda' to be of much help, leaving John with a distinct aftertaste of peace signs, Jefferson Airplane and burning joss sticks.

Colin Wilson's *The Occult*, provided a wonderful chapter on spiritualism in which seemingly approved ectoplasmic sightings and manifestations were recorded; but the book offered no suggestions as to where one might go to carry out further investigations.

Soon, John's meager collection of 'alternative' textbooks was exhausted and he took to haunting the used bookstores scattered around the Hamptons.

The days drifted by and, while autumn secured its grip on the world, John rummaged around old pasteboard shelves in musty backrooms.

By now, he had resigned his position with the design agency in East Hampton. The agency's early commiserations had given way, initially to profound understanding and then to open impatience at his continued non-appearance. John guessed the call he made from a public callbox in Westhampton, with a *Big Mac* in one hand and a collection of change in the other, came at just the right time and neatly pre-empted the agency's decision to 'let him go'.

The pay-off was generous and it meant that he could indulge himself for some time before he had to look for a new position. By then, he hoped, he would have sorted things out.

Although that happy stage was still some way off, John had made some significant discoveries. Not least of these was a series of constant references to an 18th Century book by Leopold Vachsimone entitled *Cyclical Cantata and Rhymic Stigmata*. The very name conjured up all the right images... not to mention a real dose of optimism.

He asked about it in several stores, stores whose interiors were almost as musty as the books they contained. The light in these strange and silent establishments came through dirty and greasy window glass and cast long shadows that seemed to move up and down and across the aisles as though with a life of their own. Eventually, as though they were old and faithful pets, those same shadows seemed to drift to a halt around the feet of unshaven proprietors — both men and women — of indeterminate age.

Most of these, when asked, had never heard of the Vachsimone book; but one, a man wearing two pairs of spectacles — one resting on the bridge of his nose and the other propped above his forehead, each fastened about his neck by colored bands — stared at him myopically for a moment and then began to chuckle. "Right down in the back there," the man said in a gravelly voice, jerking a nicotine-stained thumb over his shoulder towards the shady recesses of the small store. "Between Abdul Alhazred's *Necronomicon* and the slipcased first edition of *The Bible*... signed by all the contributors."

The message was clear: the book did not exist.

But on an overcast and rainy afternoon less than one week later, in a tiny store in the equally tiny village of Baiting Hollow less than a mile from the Sound, a middle-aged woman who insisted John call her Greta directed him to a cupboard beneath the staircase, its doors jammed closed by a mixture of swollen wood and neglect, suggesting he might find something in there of interest: 'her Frank', she told John, was 'into all that kind of stuff... mysticism and reincarnation and stuff'.

Continuing to itemize her late husband's interest in literary obscurities and collectibles (and all of his other foibles, shortcomings and inadequacies), the woman explained to John that she was all alone in the world — her two daughters having moved away and all but abandoned her — and that she missed 'having a man around the place'.

By the time John had forced open the doors, the woman was crouching next to him: he could smell her perfume. And by the time he had pulled out the dusty boxes, each one covered with the corpses of flies and spiders whose spindly legs were tucked up around their bellies like partially-clenched hands, the woman had rested an arm on his shoulder 'to steady herself'. Now he could smell her breath, the deep-rooted aroma of bourbon covered over — unsuccessfully — with peppermints.

The boxes contained little of interest — just a parade of titles that were either all too familiar to John or whose contents meant nothing at all to him... not so much a collection more an abandonment of books whose boards were marked and bumped, their pages foxed, dog-eared and stained with long-forgotten food dropped by long-forgotten owners.

He was about to get up and leave — as quickly as he was able, considering the woman's increasing boldness — when, lifting the re-filled boxes back into the cupboard, he saw a bundle over by the side wall, covered in bubble-wrap.

As he unfolded the wrapping to expose a single leather-covered volume, John could see the book's title and it was all he could do to keep from whooping for joy. Instead, allowing the woman to lean in against him for a closer look, he flicked through the pages and made noises of vague interest.

"I'll tell you what... Greta," he said to the woman, turning to face her as he waved Leopold Vachsimone's fabled tome in front of her nose, "I'd like to take this one — it may be useful, maybe not — but I'd like to come back sometime and take a look at what else you've got." He allowed his left eyebrow to raise slightly to emphasize the ambiguity of that statement. The woman was delighted and insisted that he 'pay her when he came back', but John, equally insistent, persuaded her to take $20. He suspected the book was worth many times that amount, but he dare not offer her more in case she suddenly decided to hold onto it and maybe offer it under auction.

The drive back home to Amagansett seemed endless and on more than one occasion John's attention was drawn to the package on the seat next to him, once again safe inside its bubble-wrap.

Back at the house, he made himself a coffee and sat down.

He opened the book at the first page and began to skim-read.

Many hours — and coffees — later he was finished. And he was excited.

He was not excited so much the book itself, which was singularly unreadable, but because of a small, folded square of lined paper which a previous owner had used as a bookmark... and had slipped into a chapter on 'Maintaining Contact With The Dead' in which much of the text had been underlined.

Most of the writing on the sheet of paper — a beautifully scrolled copperplate — had been rendered almost unreadable by age but one section of tightly-written script concerning seance-handling and 'physical contact across the void' (which close investigation showed had been copied from the two pages between which he had discovered the sheet) was as clear as though it had been written only yesterday — and right in the middle of it was a name and address: Hannah Gurding, 224 Blake Avenue, Southampton.

He slammed the book shut and punched the air, an older version of Macauley Culkin: he may be 'home alone' right now, he thought, but he wouldn't be for long.

* * *

(5)
"Everything's going to be okay, honey," he told Helen. But

his wife maintained the silence she had displayed for the two days since her return.

He wondered if that silence should be interpreted as a negative

no it isn't going to be okay, John, and you know it. You've set some wheels in motion here and the cart just isn't going to stop because you tell it

but he kept thinking that Helen had not said anything to him since he had brought her back. Or rather since Hannah Gurding had brought her back.

Sitting in the car watching the rain fall, the side window rolled down a little to let in the cool fall air, John concentrated his attention on the road ahead.

It was the second time he had traveled up to Montauk Point, the very tip of Long Island, where the Atlantic meets the coastline and the easterly winds buffet anyone fool enough to be there into a stony and silent submission.

He replayed the events that had led to that first journey.

The man who was now living at 224 Blake Avenue in Southampton — the address on the sheet of paper — did not know any Hannah Gurding. Even worse was the fact that he had lived at that address since the early 1960s. But, he suggested, maybe the guy in the General Store might know.

The guy in the General Store didn't know diddly but his mother did. His mother was one of those old women who gave off an air of quiet resignation, a misty-eyed acceptance of anything and everything that usually characterizes fervent Churchgoers who believed

The Lord works in mysterious ways

that everything that happened happened for a reason and so took all of life's little curve balls — and even the occasional skull-crunching beanie   in their stride.

Cecelia Brindle was a born-and-bred Southamptonite, she proudly proclaimed, and held cherished memories of the old days when the big houses had maids and servants, and big parties with striped tents on the lawns. And she knew all about Hannah Gurding. She laughed and shook her head when she said the woman's name — which she did a couple of times, like it was a mantra — lifting a clawlike hand, scrupulously clean but heavily liver-spotted and wattled like an old turkey's neck, up to her mouth.

"Folks hereabouts didn't take to her," the ancient woman told John. "Didn't take to her *ways*." The word 'ways' was almost spat out, like a piece of gristle in an otherwise succulent mouthful of meat.

Although he only wanted to know where Hannah Gurding was now, John couldn't let that go by without asking what the woman meant. (And, anyway, he was scared that she was going to tell him that he was wasting his time — that Hannah Gurding was long dead

Just like your missus

and pushing up the bluebonnets.)

"Oh," came the reply, with a disdainful wave of the hand and a barrage of head-shaking and *tsk-tsk-ing*, "the seance things-" She pronounced it 'say-yance', stretching out the syllables into two separate words. "-and all the noises and stuff. Thought she could speak with the departed... but," she added, with a knowing smile, "there's only God can speak with them that's gone over."

Fighting off the urge to cross himself *(spectacles, testicles, wallet and watch)* and shout '*And it's a big Amen to that, sister!*', John considered asking about the noises. But instead he said, "Where is she now? Is she... is she dead?"

Cecelia Brindle shrugged. "Left Southampton in '57, maybe '58?" She thought for a few seconds, those watery eyes twinkling as she fast-framed the sequence of events in her head. "No, it was '57. Year I turned 50."

John thought about congratulating her but felt

'tain't me y'ought to be congratulatin', son, it's the Good Lord

it would be wasted. Instead, he asked again if she knew where Hannah Gurding might be now, if she was still alive.

"Up around Montauk Point," came the answer. "And, you ask me, even that isn't far enough. Not by a long ways."

* * *

(6)

The Montauk area, the eastern tip of Long Island which culminates in Montauk Point, is as bleak as it is beautiful.

It is the end of civilization — just ten miles of crags, hills, scrub pines and glacial kettle holes regularly shrouded in fog and the air always tasting of salt. And in the middle of it was a small, two-story wooden building which overlooked the sea. This was the home of Hannah Gurding.

The first time John had gone up to Montauk, driving along State Road 27, was a late October morning.

Right from the start it always looked like it was going to be a good day, with things stacking up right and falling into place like jigsaw pieces. But even the best-looking weather can hide a storm.

Hannah Gurding's home looked like something out of a TV western — the old black and white ones, like *The Virginian* or *Bonanza*, before the TV and movie people fell in love with reality.

John pulled up on the parking area in front of the house right next to an ancient sawed-off tree trunk with a long-handled ax sitting square in the middle of the exposed whorls like Excalibur. Getting out of the car, he wondered what kind of an old woman cut her own wood... and just for a second, he wished maybe he'd told someone he was coming up here. But only for a second.

The door opened before he got anywhere near to it and the flesh-and-blood version of the little old cartoon lady who used to look after Tweety Pie appeared, rubbing her hands on a floral full-smock pinafore. She beamed a big smile and nodded, lifting a freshly-dried hand to shield her eyes from the watery sunshine.

"You either need help pretty bad or you just took the worst wrong turn in history," she said in a strong but tremulous voice. "And you don't look like that bad a driver."

John shook his head and allowed the smile to break all over his face. He nodded and shrugged, lost for words.

"Well, come on in and tell me all about it. There's fresh coffee."

He did and there was.

Over two cups of mocha you could have stood a spoon in (luckily, John wasn't sleeping anyway otherwise he'd have had an insomnia like to re-write the textbooks), he told Hannah Gurding all about Helen and about the tiny split-cells that had eventually gobbled up her brain and half of her chest, like a monstrous version of the old *PacMan* video game.

And, his mouth filled with freshly-baked hot cinnamon biscuits, he spluttered the long-drawn-out details of his hunt for the means to talk to his wife again. But more than that, he told her, watching her settle back in her high-armed fireside chair, he had promised Helen that he would bring her back.

All the while the old woman nodded, occasionally looking down into her cup, swishing whatever remained around and around, before returning her full attention to John's story.

When he finished and pulled in a deep sigh, the woman nodded and sat forward in the chair. "That it?"

"That's it," he said.

"Well, son, I can't help you."

"Can't or won't?"

She smiled and got to her feet. "Won't."

And that's when it happened.

The cumulative effect of the days and weeks of searching poured out like old dishwater. Did she know — he asked her — what it was like to lose someone who you didn't simply love but without whom you just could not contemplate the prospect of life? Without daring to pause for her to shake her head, he went on.

He told the old woman — who, when he was a boy, John had used to watch taking a broom to Sylvester the cat — all about the smell of Helen that still remained in the apartment, the lingering aroma of her perfume and her shampoo, even just her skin... of seeing her clothes still lying on the chair... of hearing her voice still on the answermachine (which he could not bring himself to erase and replace)... of how sometimes, when at last he was close to falling asleep, he thought he heard her moving around in another room and then, just when — for the tiniest of nano-seconds — he thought about wandering in to her to throw his arms around her waist and breathing in the smell of the soft skin behind her neck, the reality of everything flooded across him and in the briefest of time-passages...

He told of how Helen got a lump and they visited the doctor and then the hospital and then the magnetic imaging doodad and then her hair went with the chemotherapy and the radiotherapy and all the vomiting and the tiredness and the man at the hospital telling them about the tumor and how maybe it was a nickel or maybe a quarter and then seeing her clear out her things and then go back into hospital amidst much bravura about when she'd be getting out again and then seeing her fall into the final sleep and hoping against all hope that the next breath wouldn't be her last (or maybe hoping that it *would*) and then of her chest suddenly falling still and the disappearance of the soft wheeze of her breath plunging his world into a never-ending void of merciless silence.

And when the little old lady came to him and took him in her arms, he leaned forward and begged into the strap of her pinafore apron, the tears rolling out of his eyes and down his cheeks and mixing with the spray from his mouth and the stringy saliva that was constantly broken by the force of his words.

"There, there," she said, patting his shoulder like

she was burping a tiny baby. "I'll try help you."

* * *

(7)

He was now just a couple of miles away. And still the memories played out in his head.

He had been expecting maybe chalked pentagrams on old polished wooden floorboards exposed by rolled-back carpets. And lots of candles — maybe a couple of black ones — and even an upside-down cross or two.

He had been expecting some foul-smelling goop on the stove — bats' wings and lizard gizzards, maybe — and possibly even the sacrificial offering of a woodchuck or a rabbit.

He had been half-expecting his host to excuse herself for a few minutes... to return decked out in a long black dress, matching cape and maybe even a conical black hat perched on top of that frizz of curly white hair.

What he had *not* been expecting was what he got.

Hannah Gurding had explained that Helen would not be the way she had been. She would be virtually incommunicative — aside from maybe a glance or two: she would certainly not speak. She would arrive in only an approximation of her own body... the way it had looked before her death. (The old woman had told John that she would never consider bringing back anyone who had died in a fire or fallen from a high building.)

The body would be a construction of starmatter, she explained, of the heart of the cosmos. "Your Helen's going to be re-built from that which lies in the heart of all of us," she told him, to which he had nodded, suddenly wondering if he were wasting his time. It was all starting to sound a little too 'New Age' for him and he half-felt he were in some cheesy *Twilight Zone* rip-off... as though, if he turned his head, he'd see good old Rod Serling standing in the corner, cigarette in hand

Submitted for your approval one John Pederson, 49 years old, widower...

but if he gave up on this, there was nothing else. This was the last chance. The final hope of all the many hopes he had endured.

Hannah Gurding removed her apron and told John to sit in the chair by the fire. Truth to tell, he was pleased to be near the warmth — the air had taken on a distinct chill since the clock had slipped over into the afternoon.

As he warmed his hands in front of the burning logs his host seated herself in the other chair, pulling a tattered-looking old book from the shelf beside her. Flipping through the pages, apparently concentrating on the contents as they sped by, she said, "You should know that what I'm about to do here is a delicate operation and one I wouldn't even attempt if your Helen had passed over much longer ago than she has."

John pulled his chair nearer and settled back. "Is it dangerous?"

Hannah made a face and shrugged. "It could be. But I think it should be okay. We'll be taking Helen from the waiting area. She'll still be there... probably still be there for another couple of weeks."

"Waiting area? Waiting for what?"

"Why, admission of course."

John didn't understand. "Admission? Isn't she already-" He waved a hand. "Isn't she already in there... wherever 'in there' is?"

The old woman seemed to find a piece of text that she wanted and opened the book fully on her lap. "A lot of people die every day," she said, without looking up. "There has to be some kind of quality control as to who does get in and who don't. Hence the waiting area."

"But she will get in?"

Now she looked up. "Do you know any reason why she wouldn't?"

"Well, no. I mean, not really." He looked down at his hands and tried to think of all the things he knew about his wife. "We did a few silly things... you know. I guess everyone does."

She shook her head, frowning. "No, I don't think so."

John nodded and felt a little silly. He was about to say something else, something about Helen's many positive traits, when Hannah chuckled.

"Forgive me, son, I'm being mischievous. I very much doubt that your Helen has done anything that would warrant her exclusion from the hereafter."

As Hannah returned her attention to the book, John asked what happened to those who didn't get in.

"They remain in the waiting area."

"Forever?"

"Forever."

"Is that... is that Hell, then?"

"Well, considering the type of people you'd have for eternal companionship, I doubt it'd be very pleasant."

John looked at the fire, watched the flames licking the wood. He lifted a long metal poker from the hearth and re-arranged the pieces before placing a couple more on the exposed embers. "So why would it be dangerous?"

"We'll be opening a door," she said, her voice soft and dreamlike.

"Try to imagine it as an airport lounge, with a lot more people than there are airplanes. Some of these folks — bad folks — have been there for hundreds of years, some maybe thousands. They're like standbys, you understand what I mean? People who're waiting for a cancellation, an empty seat... or maybe a... whatchacallit? an upgrade from standard to business class. When we open that door, we have to make sure we don't allow any of them bad folks to leave at the same time. But it shouldn't really be a problem when we're only opening the door to bring someone *out*. It's a mite more delicate when you're putting someone back in."

"Where would they go... I mean, if someone were to get out?"

"Here," she said. "Where we're bringing your wife."

She closed the book. "Now, if you would be silent for a moment..."

John tented his fingers and watched the old woman through them. She closed her eyes and seemed to be muttering something under her breath, her eyelids flickering as though in REM sleep.

She opened her eyes and smiled at him. "Okay, John Pederson, get yourself over here and take a hold of my hand."

He walked across the room, crouched down beside Hannah Gurding's chair and took hold of her hand. She nodded to him and gave a big smile before resting her head against the back of the chair again.

And then it happened.

At first, John thought it was an earthquake... that maybe the Atlantic was about to engulf Montauk Point and Hannah Gurding's little two-story house, and that all of his worries and fears had been unnecessary: he was going to be seeing Helen again anyway... only at 'her place' instead of his (and his only problem would be having to explain to her how come he was arriving at the Pearly Gates with an old woman hanging onto his hand).

But then it passed and, as it passed, there was a loud crash from the old woman's kitchen.

"What was that?"

"Let's go take a look-see," she said, pulling her hand free and sounding almost casual as she got to her feet.

The first thing John noticed as he followed the old woman to the doorway leading onto the kitchen was not his wife but the gaping hole in the side wall, wooden planks and boards splintered as though a fireball had blown through them and the deep green of the grass in the yard appearing incongruous against the remains of the wall, waving in the gentle cool breeze and the gathering darkness of the afternoon.

Littered around the floor were pots and pans and

one or two pieces of crockery, remarkably unbroken despite the tiled surface. On the pine tops of the waist-high wall units other utensils were scattered and here there had been some breakages — two long-handled mugs were lying amidst shards of pottery, their sides split (Hannah *tsk-tsked* when she saw these, lifting them up and shaking her head)— while a basket whose obvious role in life was to house salad items now had some unusual guests in the shape of knives and forks from the upturned container on the shelf above.

Helen was standing against the far wall, the doorway leading outside behind her. She was staring at the shattered boards in the wall across from her.

"Oh my God," John said.

His wife was naked and painfully thin — 71-pounds-thin. She looked like one of the inmates from the concentration camps on the programmes on the History Channel, the only difference being that she was in color, not black and white.

"I take it she had lost a lot of weight," Hannah Gurding said. "By the time the end came along, I mean."

John nodded. "Is she hurt?"

"She don't appear to be."

The truth was that Helen Pederson didn't appear to be even aware of what was going on or where she was. She simply stood there, displaying no signs of modesty and showing no reaction to the cold air blowing into the kitchen.

"I'll get her something to wear," the old woman said, and she backed up past John and left the kitchen.

John walked over to her — didn't rush, as he would have expected to have done; didn't jump over to her and throw his arms around her; didn't even burst into thankful tears — and he placed a hand on her shoulder. It felt cold to the touch. There was no life there and she showed no sign of feeling the hand or even of his being in the room with her at all.

"Are you... are you okay?" he asked at last, immediately cringing at the sheer stupidity of the question but he was unable to think what else

Hi dear... have a good trip?

he could say. It suddenly seemed so long since he had last seen her. He moved his hand over her shoulder, trying to feel the bone beneath, but he couldn't feel anything although she did seem to be solid.

"Remember she's just a made-up version of what she once was," Hannah said coming back into the room with a flurry of clothes hanging over her arm. "The starmatter mixes with the soul's memory and fashions a human-like structure as close as possible to how she was when she died." She helped Helen into the things, lifting her foot to get pants on her legs and her arms to pull on a sweater. "She's not flesh and bone, or anything else that we associate with normal people."

When Helen was fully (if unfashionably) clothed, Hannah turned around. "Like I told you, you'll not get very much out of her."

"No chance of her speaking at all?"

Hannah shook her head. "Speech would mean vocal cords and larynx and spit, not to mention lungs. All she is really is a store-window mannequin. She looks the way you remember her and she is your wife... but now her soul is drawn to the hereafter. Think of her as a fish brought out of the water and expected to perform normally — the change in her environment won't harm her but neither will it mean very much to her."

"Then why have you brought her back to me?"

The old woman reached out and took hold of John's hand. "Because you asked me to," she said. "What would you have said if I'd've refused? If I'd've told you that, while I was able to do what you asked, I wouldn't do it?"

John didn't say anything.

"Some people take well to grief," she said as John watched his wife. "That's not to say that they enjoy it but only that they're better able to cope with it. In your case, you were getting worse as the weeks rolled by, not better." She gave a sad smile. "You were getting worse even as you were talking to me."

The old woman moved past him into the room.

"You need to go now. Take Helen home with you and come to terms with her passing. When you're able, bring her back to me and I'll let her go."

"What if I don't want that? What if I want to keep her?"

"We'll see," she said. Was that the hint of a slight smile playing on the corners of her mouth?

At least Helen was able to walk, but only when John took her arm and led her slowly out to the Dodge. He sat her in the front passenger seat and wrapped blankets around her knees.

"She isn't cold — unlike some of us," Hannah said, pulling an old coat around her own shoulders. "She don't feel the things that we feel — she just *feels* cold because"

"I know; because she hasn't any blood and hasn't any heart." Realizing that he had snapped, John apologized.

"That's okay. You're absolutely right. Never apologize for being right, son, only for being wrong."

As he got into the car, John said, "I'll pay for the damage to your kitchen. Just get it fixed and let me know the cost."

She waved him nevermind although, watching the car pull away, there was something in what the young fella had said that suddenly gave her a frisson of unease.

It wasn't until she had got inside, made a fresh pot of coffee, put some more logs on the low fire and set about clearing up the mess that she realized why: the wreckage from the smashed wall was all *outside* the house. It had not been caused by something coming *in* but by something going *out*.

She looked out into the wind and the encroaching twilight, her eyes skimming the distant woods and lonely forest trails, and wondered where that something was.

And *what* it was.

Hannah Gurding never regretted things generally, but at that moment she wished she had a telephone.

* * *

(8)

Although it was an automotive development with which he was not familiar, the Eldorado's automatic transmission was a big help to the man who looked like Solomon Grundy out of the old Batman comicbooks.

It had been a long time since he had driven a car — his last one had been a 1929 Model A Tudor sedan — and it was enough for him simply to have to concentrate on steering the thing without having to shift a gear lever as well.

He had no real idea where he was going, only that he must follow the trail of glittering dust that drifted languidly up into the sky and stretched far ahead of him into the darkness. But if that darkness had not been there and he had been able to make out the surroundings, he might have realized that he had passed this way once before, albeit on foot and in the opposite direction... he might even have recognized the spot where, in a ditch at the bottom of a scrub-covered ravine, he had left a small man clothed only in his shirt, shorts and socks, face down in the mud, his neck twisted around and snapped like kindling.

But he was concentrating on the road ahead and on keeping on it; the window was down and the wind was blowing against his face... although he was not aware of it. Nor was he aware any more of the trail of fairy dust he himself was leaving behind him, trailing out into the October night sky like soap bubbles.

Meanwhile, just a few miles and minutes in front of him, John Pederson was pulling his car up outside Hannah Gurding's house at Montauk Point, feeling suddenly lighter of heart. Certainly much lighter of heart than he had been when he had left here two days earlier.

He looked across at his passenger and patted her knee.

"Everything's going to be okay," he said.

But it wasn't.

In fact, *nothing* was going to be okay.

* * *

(9)

For two whole days, John had tried to get some kind of reaction from his wife... or, at least, an acknowledgment of who he was or even *who* she was. But there was nothing.

She sat only when he led her to the sofa and bent her into a seated position. Then she just stayed in whatever position he left her in, not moving, showing no emotion.

He showed her photographs of the two of them together, telling her where the shot was taken and how wonderful it had been; he brought articles of her clothing — her favorite clothing — proudly placing them on her lap, explaining carefully and quietly and slowly what each particular item was and how much she had loved wearing it; and, most of all, he kept speaking to her, all the time, telling her how they would be happy again... once she had learned to adapt.

Late at night, when he was sure that they would not see anyone they knew — and, more importantly, that nobody they knew would see *them* (and so discover what he had done) — he took Helen out into the smoky October streets of Amagansett, looking in the store windows and sitting on the park benches watching the night sky.

By the middle of the day after he had brought Helen back home, John knew that he had made a bad judgment call.

If he had been able to bring his wife back into his life — *really* bring her back, just the way she had been — then everything would have been fine. But the Helen that sat around the apartment, silently watching (if she *was* watching or even registering anything at all), was not his wife. She was a stranger.

The first inclination of this inescapable fact was when, on the evening of the day he had brought her home, John had helped remove Helen's clothes, wincing at the almost skeletal thinness of her body

the starmatter mixes with the soul's memory and fashions a human-like structure as close as possible to how she was when she died

and maneuvered her into the bed they once shared.

He had slipped into the other side of the bed, pulling the sheets carefully up around them, and he had snuggled up against her the way he had always snuggled up against her. She was cold, cold and alien... like a piece of dead meat, a carcass that did not think, did not respond, did not feel and, most of all, did not live. There was no movement, no fidgeting, no pulse or heartbeat.

The new Helen did not eat — she sat, almost dutifully, staring at him and even through him, a plate of fries and a piece of grilled fish before her on the table, while John picked at his own food, hardly tasting anything, unable to work up the saliva needed even to chew.

The new Helen did not even blink — he had noticed that early in the evening when, as an experiment, he sat and watched her face without speaking, staring at her eyes as they, in turn, seemed to stare at him. There was no movement at all.

Then, on the afternoon of what would have been the second full day of their post-mortem life together, John went out to the store, explaining to a disinterested Helen that they needed things — which they didn't — and that maybe she could watch a little television while he was gone. He turned on the television and tuned it to a channel showing a talk show in which incredibly fat people were invited by the host to explain their problems to a supposedly caring audience. John imagined an edition of the same show in which the guests were all people who had tried to bring their deceased relatives back to life: for a second or two, he could almost see the situation on the screen, the

73

would-be resurrections seated along the back of the stage, with their dead-eyed loved ones lined up in front of them on a lower level, the ravages of the cancers, embolisms, cardiac arrests, plane wrecks and muggings hanging from their pallid skin...

Once outside, John looked back at the house wondering whether, now that she was on her own, Helen might come across to the window of her own volition and take a look outside. But she didn't. There was only the intermittent brightness of the TV screen, its flickering images washing over the store-window dummy seated in front of it, its hands clasped obediently in its lap, thinking — if it were capable of thinking at all — only dead thoughts.

Walking along the streets, not wanting to go anywhere and not wanting to go back, John decided that he had made a mistake.

He who never makes a mistake never makes anything, his father used to say. John wondered what his father or his mother, both of them dead these past eight and seventeen years respectively, would make of what he had done. Hannah Gurding had been right — he would take Helen back... release her.

The decision, when it came, lifted a colossal weight from his shoulders.

Maybe when he told her, Helen would respond gratefully.

This had been a bad idea right from the start, he decided, heaping new rationalities onto the small building blocks of common sense he had just laid. But maybe he had needed to do it. Yes, that made sense. Some folks could cope better with the grief of loss — even Hannah Gurding had said so. There was no stigma attached to it. He had needed to go through this as a cathartic process.

Then, with the house once again in sight in the gathering darkness, all of those thoughts disappeared like rain on parched summer ground. There was no light flickering in the window — the television had been turned off.

Hardly daring to think, John broke into a run. Helen was going to be okay — she had turned off the shlocky talkshow and all the fat people: Christ, she had more sense as an ex-dead person than most of the still-living population.

Then he saw the front door. It was open.

Then he saw that it was not merely open but *smashed* open

like the wall in Hannah Gurding's kitchen

with splinters of wood strewn on the hall carpet. There was something about that wreckage that made him feel suddenly nervous — something apart from the fact that it was there at all... it was something else.

He ran into the house calling his wife's name — ignoring what the neighbors would think if they heard him, his wife having been dead these past few weeks — and didn't know whether to be dismayed that there was no response at all. He turned left into the main room and stopped dead in his tracks. Helen was still there, facing the television, just the way he had left her. As he had already deduced from outside, the television was no longer on. But that wasn't because Helen had turned it off. She had smashed it.

"Jesus Christ, what have you *done*?" He kept his voice low so that he didn't panic her. "Why didn't you just-"

He stopped when he turned around and saw the room door, drunkenly hanging from its top hinge; then he saw the smashed table, the one where he had placed their meals and from which he had removed Helen's untouched plate; and he saw the drapes, pulled from the runner across the top of the windows. He looked back at Helen. She had not moved since he had returned.

John moved into the center of the room and crouched in front of her. His wife's eyes did not move, did not register him at all. She was sitting just the way she had been sitting when he had left. Exactly the same position.

"It wasn't you at all, was it, honey," he said.

Looking around the room, John couldn't see anything missing. Whoever had done this had apparently been intent on simply smashing the place up — and, he had to admit, they'd done a pretty good job.

Maybe he should report it. But who to? To the police? Or just the insurance company? They'd ask questions — questions like was anyone there?

Well, just my dead wife

Okay, that wasn't a problem. He would lie. Nobody was there — come to think of it, it wasn't much of a lie. But, if he reported it to the police, what if they caught the guy? And then the guy confessed everything but happened to mention

... there was this broad, just sittin in the room... you know wadda mean? Just sittin there while I fuckin totaled it — you hear what I'm saying here...

about Helen — that would not be good. He could imagine his explanation — *Yes, well, I did this 'Bell, Book and Candle' routine with an old biddy up in Montauk Point, and she... well, she brought my wife back from the dead (you hear what I'm sayin' here...).* So, no police.

That's when he looked across at the telephone, saw the flashing light which signified a message.

"Somebody call, honey?" he said as he walked across to the phone.

Helen didn't respond.

He pressed the message button and the metallic voice said *You have two messages* while the machine rewound the tape.

Hi, you've reached John and Helen, the old Helen Pederson said: *we're not in right now or can't get to the phone... but leave us a message and we'll get back to you. Here comes the beep...*

"Was that Helen?" Hannah Gurding asked. "Mister Pederson, if you're there, please pick up the phone." There was a pause. Then, "Okay, you're not there. Mister

Pederson, it's Hannah Gurding?" She paused, giving him time (as if he needed it) to place the name.

"I think we... *you* have a problem," Hannah's voice continued. "And it's a biggie. You recall the smashed wall at my house? Well, it was smashed from the *in*side, not the outside. Helen wasn't *alone*, is what I'm trying to tell you. She brought somebody back with her, somebody from the waiting area. That person is out there, *some*where, right now. And he or she will know that the only person standing in their way-"

The machine clicked and the metallic voice explained that the message came in at 2.47 PM.

Helen's voice echoed around the room once more and John closed his eyes, fighting back the tears.

"It's Hannah Gurding again," Hannah Gurding's voice said.

As soon as she started speaking, John could hear a doppleganger of her voice, in the conversation of two days earlier.

... imagine it as an airport lounge...

"You need a longer tape, Mister Pederson... and you need to change your answering machine message there..."

...with a lot more people than there are airplanes. Some of those people have been there for hundreds of years...

"... need to bring Helen back," Hannah was saying. "Now, Mister Pederson. Whoever's out there will know that the only way they can be made to return to the waiting area is for the person they came with to be returned...

... like standbys, you understand what I mean? People who are waiting for a cancellation, an empty seat... or maybe an upgrade from standard to business class...

"... and the only person who can make that happen is *you*. If you are out of the way, they can stay. It's complicated, I accept..."

... we must make sure we don't allow any others to leave at the same time. But it shouldn't really be a prob-

lem when we're bringing someone out...

"... but I hope I'm making myself clear here. You are in the most *extreme* danger. This is a very delicate and very complex situation. You have to bring Helen back *immediately*." She hung up the phone.

The machine said that the message had been placed at 2.51 PM.

It was 3.12.

John and Helen were in the Dodge at 3.18 — it took him that long to lead Helen out of the house — and backing out onto the street as the digital display kicked over to 19.

As he pulled into the light traffic leading down to Main Street and the State Road, one thing was re-playing in John's mind: what exactly had Hannah meant when she had said

... shouldn't really be a problem when we're only bringing someone out!

that last bit? He wasn't too sure that he liked the emphasis on that final word... purely because they were no longer going to try to do that. This time they were going to try putting somebody back in. And hadn't she said something about that?

By the time they got through Main Street and saw the first sign for State Road 27, it was 3.39 and already getting quite dark.

John had a feeling it was going to get even darker before it was over.

* * *

(10)
Hannah Gurding flung open her front door and stood drying her hands. Despite the situation he was in, John wondered what on earth the old woman could be doing every time someone came calling that caused her to have to wipe her hands, but he suspected it was simply an affectation.

"Quickly," she shouted into the wind, "bring her inside and let's get this thing started." She looked around, still wiping ferociously. "I can smell rain," she said. "Think mebbe there's a storm a coming." With a quick glance down the road he had just driven, she turned around and disappeared into the house.

Getting Helen moving was not the easiest thing in the world, and certainly not the fastest. But, eventually, John had managed to maneuver his wife out of the car and was leading her through the front door.

Somewhere in the distance — not yet near but not all that far away — thunder rolled menacingly and the doorway was momentarily bathed in light.

The room looked just the way it had looked on his previous visit. The same sense of pleasant clutter, a room that looked lived in.

Hannah was in the kitchen, drying her hands again — this time on a small towel with a picture of a man fishing emblazoned in its center. John noticed that she had propped some wooden boards against the hole in the outside wall: when he looked down to see if the debris had also been cleared he suddenly realized that that was what had seemed wrong when he had got home to all the debris of his own house — there hadn't *been* any debris in Hannah Gurding's kitchen. If he'd realized that earlier, maybe a lot of this could have been avoided. But the woman — Hannah herself — had noticed. That was something. *Wasn't* it?

"Where should I–" He glanced at his wife, suddenly aware that he was speaking about her in front of her but her blank expression reminded him that such social courtesies were unwarranted. "Where do you want me to put her?" he asked, finishing the question.

"Anywhere." Hannah came bustling back into the room and pointed to the sofa by the side wall. "Sit her down over there. She'll be fine."

She walked across to the door and turned the key. Then she slid along a thick bolt beneath it, and another at the very top of the door.

"Where do you want me to go?"

The old woman strode quickly to the fireside chair and plopped down into it. "Where you were last time, but I'll need you to come over to me again. And this time, you'll need to be holding your wife's hand when you make contact with me." She took a deep breath and picked up a thick book from beside the chair. As she flicked through the pages, she glanced over at John. "You okay?"

He nodded and shuddered. "Why didn't he — whoever he is-"

"Or she is," Hannah corrected, concentrating her attention on the open book. "There's women bad as well as men."

"It's a 'he'. We — *I* — saw him, down in Amagansett. Tried to stop the car... beat up some people — killed them for all I know..." John shook his head. The whole thing sounded ridiculous. "And then a car hit him. Knocked him down-" He clapped his hands together. "-and then he got up. just as though nothing had happened."

"Nothing *had* happened," she said. "Don't forget, he's not flesh and blood like you and me. No veins or arteries, no heart or organs. It's just a vessel housing his soul. That's all. You can't kill a soul," she said.

John was suddenly reminded of the line in the *Halloween* movie, where Jamie Lee Curtis tells one of the kids that the person who had been causing all the carnage was the Boogie Man. *Where is he now?* the kid asks. *He's dead,* Curtis replies. The kid shakes his head, looking scared. *But you can't kill the Boogie Man*, he says.

"So why didn't he..." John nodded across at Helen.

"The people in the waiting area can't hurt each other."

"But she's solid, whatever else she is... and he's solid enough to have trashed my house."

She sat up in the chair. "He came to your house? You see him?"

John shook his head. "He came while I was out. Smashed everything up." He looked across at Helen to see if she was responding but the face he had loved — still *did* love — so deeply was completely blank. "Left her sitting there just the way I'd left her," he went on, "watching the television."

"We don't have time to chat about things," she said. "I'm not even sure myself all the whys and wherefores... suffice to say they don't even *touch* each other, let alone try to do harm. It's the way things are." She shrugged.

John turned sharply to look at the window. He had thought he had heard a car — seen its headlights wash over the room through the windows — but, as he turned, a deep rumble sounded somewhere out to sea. Just thunder and lightning. The storm was getting closer.

"So he's out there somewhere, looking for you," Hannah said.

In the momentary silence between thunderclaps there was a crunch from outside the house, over by the window.

Then lightning flashed and the heavens rumbled.

John tried to relax. "He can't be here," he said, not sounding very convinced. "He doesn't even know where we are."

"He can follow the starmatter."

"Starmatter? *What* starmatter?"

"The stuff that makes us all up — with them, it's more noticeable because their new bodies are not 'tainted' by all the things that go to make up humans." She patted her stomach. "The things we nurture in our bellies for getting on nine months... gizzards, innards, spit and vinegar. With them it's only the scrapings of the cosmos. And their soul deep inside. Nothing more. And as they walk around — or even just sit — tiny bits of it fly off, trying to get back out there to where it came from."

John frowned. "*I* never saw anything."

"You wouldn't. But somebody else from up there would," she said, rolling her eyes to the ceiling.

"So, if we just left her — or one of them — they'd eventually just disappear?"

81

She nodded. "But not in our lifetime. Not even in the next generation's lifetime... maybe not even the one comes after."

He twisted his fingers around each other. "Well, I didn't see any floating starmatter."

"I just told you, *you* can't see- ah, got it!" She closed the book with a thud. "We're in business."

Thunder rolled again but it had finished before it could conceal the crunching noise outside. This time, Hannah looked up. "He's here."

John would never have believed that two short words could carry such impact.

He had heard or read about how fear had frozen a person in their tracks but here it was really happening... not in a book, not in a movie.

John looked across at the old woman and saw something flicker behind the lines on her face, rolling beneath her skin like maggots feeding. Fear. Hannah Gurding was frightened and that made John very frightened.

He leaned close to her, pulling gently on Helen's arm, tugging her across with him so that it looked like the three of them were hatching plans... only Helen wasn't hatching anything. Helen was just staring as she always stared, watching the wall across from them.

"What do we do?"

"We move quickly is what we do," Hannah replied. She tugged the book open on her lap and, keeping a hold of John's right hand, began flicking through looking for something. John hoped she knew what it was she was looking for. He didn't like the way she was muttering under her breath, each of her little phrases sounding like they had question marks at the end of them, making it sound like she didn't know what she was doing. John didn't like the idea of that. He didn't think they had time to not know what they were doing.

Something fell to the floor in the kitchen, clattering, its echoes sounding hollow and empty.

"He's coming in," John said. "Can he get in?"

Without pausing in the flicking, Hannah said, "He can do anything he's a mind to do."

John shuffled sideways so that he had a better view of the damaged kitchen wall. He wished he hadn't. It looked like it wouldn't keep out Scooby Doo let alone a psychotic zombie-thing hell-bent on making sure it didn't get repatriated.

"Here," she said, "I think this is what we need."

"I think what we need is

how 'bout Superman, Schwarzenegger and Bruce Willis?

to move as quickly as we can," John said, trying to keep the panic out of his voice but feeling it bubble up his throat like soda-bile.

"Okay," she said. "Behind the sofa." She got to her feet and momentarily stepped in front of John so that he couldn't see the kitchen.

He pushed her to the side and craned his neck to see. Was that movement on the pieces of board? And what had caused the thing to clatter in there? He swallowed deeply and noisily. Maybe the thing was already in there... maybe it had found another way into the-

"Is there another way into the kitchen?"

Hannah shook her head. "Quickly, behind the sofa."

John frowned and did a double take at his wife, half-expecting her to chuckle at his expression. The old woman's suggestion sounded like those civil defense instructions where, if an 'A-tomic Bomb' were to drop, folks should just get behind a chair or maybe stand behind the door. Just like airliner passengers putting their heads between their legs in case of a crash. John figured St. Peter always knew when a bunch of folks from an air crash wound up at the Pearly Gates because they all had their heads stuck up their asses.

"What'll that do?"

"Give us time." She stepped over the chair arm and

pulled the sofa away from the wall. John got to the other side and pulled that out, too.

Something groaned in the kitchen. John knew straight away what it was: it was the sound of a board creaking against a nail, complaining about being jimmied.

"Get her down at that end," Hannah whispered, pointing, "and you get next to her. I'll stay at this end — it'll be easier for me to get in here.

John moved around to the end of the sofa and shuffled along behind it, pulling Helen in after him. While he helped maneuver his wife into a crouching position, he kept his eyes on the kitchen. Nothing was moving. Everything had gone quiet again and no boards were doing any complaining.

As he hunkered next to Helen, his back sliding down the wall, John's eyes scanned the wall at the far end of the room, taking it all in for the first time as though his brain was grasping for idle thoughts to calm itself.

Right next to the kitchen doorway on a patch of blank wall hung a painting of the outside of a barn, an upended pail in the foreground and the shadowy recesses of the barn interior hovering in the back. It looked like it could be an original. Next to that, on a listing shelf that had seen better days, an old radio sat amidst a mess of books, looking like it could get Orson Welles laughing his Lamont Cranston laugh just by flicking the dial. Now more than ever before, John Pederson too knew what evil lurked in the heart of man.

And right next to that, caught full in the center of the window between two garishly floral curtains — one slightly longer than the other (John noticed idly) — was an ax head; and right next to that was the profile of Solomon Grundy. He did not appear to be happy.

John ducked quickly behind the sofa just in time to see Hannah Gurding crawl in at the other end on her hands and knees.

"Did he see us?" John hissed, wanting to speak

louder so that the old woman could hear him over the tom-tom beat of his heart.

"Who?" she whispered. Seeing the incredulity on John's face, she added, "Where is he?"

"Outside the window."

"What was he doing?"

John didn't answer. He listened, expecting to hear a monstrous growl as the man burst through the wall in a shower of wood shards and glass splinters

Fee Fi Fo Fum, I smell the blood of a dead woman...

... to hear the clumsy half-asleep clump of his Karloff feet as he moved across to the sofa with his ax.

"Can you hear anything?" Hannah asked.

John shook his head. He turned to Helen and patted the hand he had been holding, suddenly realizing he had been gripping it like a vise. He tried to conjure up a smile but it came out as a sneer. Helen just stared.

"Okay," Hannah said, "give me your hand again."

John did as she asked.

"Now, sit real quiet while I concentrate."

"What... what did you mean when you said... when you said it wouldn't be too difficult if we were only, you know... only pulling someone out and–"

She was staring at the book on the floor and muttering.

Something thumped against the door. Then thumped again.

The door shook in its frame.

Hannah kept muttering.

John scrunched his head down into his neck, hardly daring to breathe.

Helen stared at the back of the sofa.

The ax clattered against the door and John heard something clunk at the other side of the room. The key. The force of the ax had shaken the key out of the door and sent it hurtling across the room.

Someone moaned and John realized it was him.
Hannah kept on muttering.
Everything had gone quiet again.
"Nearly there," Hannah said, closing the book.
John edged upwards, running his nose up against the musty-smelling material of the sofa, until his forehead was suddenly free. His eyes followed close behind it.
The room was exactly as they had left it, only now it looked strangely alien... like they had no place in being there.
Solomon Grundy was staring through the window. Staring right at John.
He ducked his head and turned to Hannah.
"He saw me." There was nothing more to be said on the matter.
They listened and heard the thing's footsteps move slowly back towards the kitchen.
"Jesus, he's comin-"
The hastily-constructed board-covering shattered... pieces of wood flying into the kitchen and hitting pots and pans, sending them clattering to the floor. John didn't like that, he suddenly realized: he didn't like it because the cacophony covered up the sound of the big man's feet.
"Another minute," Hannah said, closing her eyes. "Keep holding onto Helen... keep holding her tight..."
John edged up again.
The boarding was almost through. The only thing that was going in their favor was that he was so slow.
He saw the ax come down, sloppily, side-on, against the boards.
Then a hand appeared, pulling at them.
Hannah said, "Hold her, I'm at the door..."
At the door? No way. The Jolly Green Golem was 'at the door'... and then John realized that the old woman was speaking of a different door. He was momentarily heartened.
Then Solomon Grundy's knee burst through.

Then a hand holding an ax.

Then a folded-up Solomon Grundy himself squeezed into the kitchen and stood up. He turned and looked at John, then looked around the kitchen.

He switched the ax to his other hand and started to walk towards him.

"He's coming..."

"I know, I know..." She muttered something under her breath and gripped John's hand tightly.

The air around them seemed to swirl, and wind buffeted their faces.

"He's coming for crissakes!"

Solomon Grundy had the ax held high. He moved with a lolling gait, catching the side of an old bureau with his hip. A trio of framed photographs of people who didn't seem to know how to smile sank to the wooden surface with a clump.

"It's open," she said, "now hold tight..."

He held as tight as he could, gripping his wife's hand and the hand of the old woman for all he was worth.

The whole house sounded like it breaking apart. John could hear things falling up above him, and he suddenly wondered what Hannah Gurding's other rooms looked like... wondered what her bedroom looked like.

The big man pulled aside the high-backed chair the old woman had been sitting on and tossed it across against the wall like it was a stage prop. The old radio rocked once and then fell in an avalanche of books and shelving, the electrical lead growing taught for a few seconds and then the plug jerking free of the socket to whiplash empty air before it followed the radio to the floor in a rumbling crash.

Thunder sounded outside, answering the primal call of the chaos in the house, and lightning flashed twice. Then another thunderclap, only this one was directly above John's head. Then it was in the kitchen and across the room... everywhere in the old house.

The man took another step, swaying slightly, and then another.

John looked down at Helen's hand. She was squeezing.

He turned to look at her, away from the sight of the big man bringing the ax down towards the sofa, hearing the old woman muttering, hearing her voice grow suddenly louder and more shrill, seeing Helen's face suddenly grow softer around the edges... seeing his wife's mouth curl into a gentle and knowing smile... seeing, in his peripheral vision, the ax... coming down now... watching his wife's other hand lift slowly from her side towards his waiting face... and he closed his eyes to wait for the impact—

When it came, it was as he imagined the Bikini Atoll tests, shaking his entire body, switching off all of the circuits and then switching them on again, then off, then on... he moved his face towards that hand, yearning for Helen's touch again, yearning for her to tell him that everything was okay.

Someone screamed.

The lights went out.

The ax dropped onto the sofa's seats — John felt it bounce twice against the springy back — and the hand in which he had been holding Helen's hand clasped shut. Empty.

He opened his eyes and stared at darkness.

Then the lights came back on.

Helen had gone.

John slowly pulled himself up from behind the sofa. The Solomon Grundy-thing wasn't there. He looked back at the empty space on his left and felt a curious emotion — part elation and part desperate sadness.

"It's done," Hannah said. "They've gone." She slumped down to a sitting position and closed her eyes.

John stepped out from behind the sofa and walked around to the other side so that he could help Hannah to her feet.

"She recognized me," he said, "at the end."

"Yes? And does that make you happy?"

He nodded. Then, remembering what the old woman had said, he frowned. "You never told me... why was this time any more dangerous than the other time?"

"This time we had to open the door and then put Helen through. That means we create a opening... a few unguarded moments when the door was open and unprotected. The first time, we just opened it, reached in and pulled Helen out through the hole, so it was covered all the time."

"But we still managed to get... him."

She shrugged. "That was just bad luck. He just got pulled along in her wake."

John nodded. It sounded as reasonable an explanation as he could hope for, under the highly unreasonable circumstances.

"And now you must go," she said. John saw her eyes drift up towards the ceiling. Was that a noise up there?

"I'm going to help you tidy-"

"No, you must leave now. Go quickl-"

Something clattered in the kitchen.

There was a creak from the wall running from the kitchen doorway to the staircase door, partway up... as though something was on the stairs.

He looked at the old woman, saw the exhaustion pull at her features. Then he looked across at the door leading to the staircase.

"I think..." Hannah began, and stopped. Her eyes moved from John's face to the kitchen doorway behind him. He turned around.

The man standing in the doorway was buck naked, his hair pulled tight around his head into a thick pony tail at the back. A wide scar ran down from his forehead, over the bridge of his nose and down his left to cheek. Where it crossed his mouth, before ending at the cleft chin, it had pulled the lips down into a permanent grimace. He had a large knife in each hand.

A shadow moved in the kitchen behind him.

The door to the staircase opened and a bald, fat man wearing a pair of long-legged pantaloon bloomers and a deep-interlaced brassiere stepped into the room, his hands on his hips. He looked like he was trying to smile but either couldn't quite get the hang of it or had forgotten how.

Shuffling noises came from the staircase, descending slowly.

Still more could be heard in the room over their heads.

John Pederson started to say he was sorry — to Hannah Gurding, to his dead and newly departed (for the second time) wife and to all of the people upon whom his mistake was going to be visited for a long time to come — but he never really got started.

* * *

(11)

When at last they emerged — through the hole in the kitchen wall because they were unable to find a key for the front door — there were eleven of them, walking slowly around the parked cars in front of the house and onto the paved roadway that led to the unsuspecting world.

Some were tall, some were short; some carried knives, others pieces of furniture or house tools; one of them had found the ax.

Some wore shoes, some were barefoot; some wore sweaters — tightly fitting — and some wore coats. And one exceptionally fat one wore an ill-fitting wig of curly, white hair. Though nobody would know by looking at him, this same one also sported a set of women's lingerie beneath the tweed coat he had pulled tightly about him.

Only two things bonded them together as a group.

The first of these — a fine, powder-like trail of twinkling dust which seemed to emanate from their heads and drift up into the night sky — could not be seen by anyone except one of their own number.

The second thing was the bloodstains, eloquently dark in the moonlight.

> **And I saw a new heaven and a new earth:**
> **for the first heaven and the first earth were passed away;**
> **and there was no more sea.**
> *Revelation, 21, 1*

The Space Between the Lines

The first person David Milligan saw after leaving his wife lying spread-eagled across the hood of the Oldsmobile was a jogger, frozen mid-step in the late-afternoon light, the man's sweat-lined face pulled into a hooded-eyed mixture of determination and discomfort.

David had been half-walking half-trotting along the blacktop that led down into Forest Plains. When he saw the jogger he figured he'd been around 15 maybe 20 minutes on the road. He realized he'd have to get a move on, though he had no idea of just how long he had left. Maybe it was an hour, maybe it was more. He worried that it might even be less. Maybe there was no specific length of time involved at all. Maybe the whole process was completely arbitrary.

For the first few minutes after leaving the wrecked car David had checked and re-checked his watch, initially skeptical and then just out-and-out incredulous — after all, it had been a long time since Uncle Alan and the episode at Bentley Grange.

Leaving the car had been the first step on a journey into another realm
there's a signpost up ahead: next stop...
signaled by the dull sound when he had slammed the buckled door of the Oldsmobile. The strong and usually heavy metallic door that suddenly felt like it had been sculpted out of polystyrene or balsa wood.

Now he was trotting again, holding the piece of dashboard tightly in his hand. He could feel the roll of tape in his pants pocket, rubbing against his leg. He glanced down at the dashboard as he ran, saw the piece of brown Scotch tape half on and half off a diagonal of shadow trapped in place on the plush fabric. He held onto the dashboard and doubled his efforts, letting his mind drift back to what his uncle had told him all those years ago.

***

"It's the space between the lines," Uncle Alan said. "That briefest of moments in which the story stops and then starts again."

David stared at him, hanging on the words. He glanced to the side and saw Richard lift a threadbare Panama hat to his mouth, the hat's weave running to holes around the turned crown. Richard tried to bite a piece out of the brim, gave it up, waved it a couple of times and then tossed it to the floor.

"Richard!" David's and Richard's father waggled a finger at Richard and then picked up the discarded hat and placed it on the table beyond Richard's reach.

"It's okay, John," Uncle Alan said in that lazy drawl of his, sounding like he was John Wayne in one of the cowboy movies that David loved so dearly. "It's only Ernest Hemingway's favorite headgear!" Uncle Alan gave a shrug and chuckled after this, winking at David when he saw David looking at him.

David's father smiled and shook his head. "It had to be Hemingway didn't it, Alan?" John Milligan said, his voice a strange mixture of tiredness and inquiry. Hemingway was David's father's favorite writer.

"Didn't have to be," Uncle Alan said softly, "but it is."

David didn't care diddly about Ernest Hemingway — particularly as Hemingway was responsible for that story about an old man trying to catch a big fish, a story John Milligan used to try to read to David but which David found very boring — but he liked the bit about spaces between lines. That sounded kind of strange, something he should know more about. He shuffled forward on his seat and stretched his arms across the table, leaning on them so that his head came right in front of Uncle Alan who was watching David's baby brother chaw his gums on a plastic key ring shaped and colored like it was a fried egg.

"Whatcha mean about spaces between lines, Uncle Alan?" David asked.

Uncle Alan's eyes refocused on David. He leaned forward, resting his head on his hands and said, "You read many books?"

David shrugged. "Some," he said. "A few," he added with another shrug. He checked his finger-ends the way he saw his father do when he didn't want to get into a discussion. But it was true. He had read *Yogi Bear Goes To College* — without much help being needed... or asked for anyways — and his Aunt Joan had read to him from something called *Gidget Goes Hawaiian*. Aunt Joan thought that the book was a real hoot but David didn't think too much to it. He even thought of mentioning the one about the old man and the fish but he decided against it because he couldn't actually remember much of it. The fact was that, mostly, he read comicbooks and, after what he decided was a long enough time studying his finger-ends, he said so to Uncle Alan.

"Comicbooks!" said Uncle Alan, thumping the table. "Why, that's even better." He got to his feet and glanced around the room until he spied the *Strange Adventures* that Danny Kobel, the kid next door back home in Cedar Rapids, had given to David in what amounted to a veritable pile of DC comics for his vacation in England. David thought that *Strange Adventures* was kind of neat, particularly as it wasn't one of his usual purchases — not like *Casper* and *Baby Huey*, or *Jerry Lewis* and *Pvt Doberman*, or even *Archie* and *Jughead*, for which David's father was always happy to shell out a few extra dimes allowance... provided he got to read them, too. In fact, those were the only times that David seemed to hear his father laughing these days, when John Milligan took the latest copy of *Jughead* or *Pals 'n' Gals* to his bedroom — the room he used to share with David's mom — and his soft chuckling filtered through the walls and along the hallways at home when David was finding it tough to get to sleep.

95

Lonesome Roads

Of course, David thinking the *Strange Adventures* was kind of neat did not necessarily mean he fully understood the story — he was still on the first one of the three tales, something about a big hand that kept appearing to protect this guy when he got into danger — but he liked the almost breathlessly dangerous fact that it took him into older kids' territory. Why, the next thing you knew, he'd be chewing gum! And still only six years old! Almost.

"Looks like a goody," Uncle Alan said, looking at the cover which showed a man and woman riding in their car over the brow of a hill with this enormous hand stretching up behind them. As Uncle Alan flicked through the gaudily-colored pages, David considered thanking him for the compliment but then decided against it. After all, it wasn't as though his uncle was congratulating David for a job well done. He hadn't done anything at all except accept the comics from Danny Kobel. David shrugged and shuffled his bottom side to side on his chair.

"So," said Uncle Alan, pulling a high-backed chair out into the center of the room and twirling it around. "The spaces between the lines... or, in this case, the spaces between the *panels*." He sat astride the chair and leaned forward so that his arms — and the comicbook — hung over the chair back.

"Panels?" David stared at the comicbook page that Uncle Alan held open before him. "What are panels?"

Richard's eighteen-month-old mind seemed to find this question immensely amusing and he chuckled loudly, tossing the fried egg key-ring across the room while slapping the table with a tiny hand as he leaned forward in his high chair.

John Milligan stepped across to his youngest son and ruffled the boy's hair affectionately. "What are they talking about, huh Rich?" he said. But then he crouched down by Richard's chair and concentrated his attention on the open comicbook.

"See now," said Uncle Alan, pointing his finger to

the first illustration on the page. "This is a panel. Watch it closely and see what happens."

David watched.

David's father watched.

The illustration showed a giant hand swatting a falling tree away from a young boy who crouched directly beneath it. In the drawing, it was raining, the rain depicted by diagonally scrawled pen marks running from the right of the picture downwards. The artist — whoever he was — must be real good because David could actually hear the rain. He could hear the sound of the water pelting the ground, could hear the boy's breathless words of surprise (captured for convenience in a word balloon above the boy's head), and he could hear the sound of timber cracking.

But best of all, the illustration was *moving*.

"It's moving!" David said, his voice scarcely above a whisper.

Richard chuckled some more and slapped the table again, this time with both hands in what amounted to a synchronized drum roll.

"How do you do that?" asked John Milligan.

"Shh," said Uncle Alan. "I'm not doing anything... not really. It's your imagination. Let it take you with it."

"Majinayshun?" David echoed.

Uncle Alan moved his finger across to the next illustration and now that too started to move... rippling like paper approaching combustion and about to burst into flames. "See, we've moved on now," Uncle Alan explained. "The boy is staring up into the sky wondering how he dare tell anyone what has happened because the hand has gone."

He moved his finger down to another illustration in which the boy, who had now grown up to be a young man, was falling from a mountainside. David gasped involuntarily. He could smell the stone and the air, could smell the clump of grass and soil crumbling beneath the man's hands as he tumbled backwards into the void below. Uncle Alan moved his finger to the final panel on the page and the hand re-appeared beneath the man. David could see the veins around the wrist, could see them moving, the muscles tensing as the hand prepared to catch the man.

Uncle Alan said, "And now watch what happens when you look only at the space between the panels." He moved his finger to the white space between the bordered illustrations.

David looked.

David's father looked.

Even Richard looked, or seemed to.

"Nothing's happening," John Milligan said, his tone suggesting that he thought the whole experiment had been a complete waste of time.

"The drawings've stopped moving," David observed.

"Absolutely right, David," said Uncle Alan. "And that is the space between the lines, the pause in the story. Nothing happens there."

Paws? David frowned. A story had *paws*? He looked around at his father and saw him shaking his head as though he were waking from a dream. That proved it. Even his dad didn't believe a story had paws.

Now his dad rubbed his mouth and half-smiled. "How do you *do* that?"

Uncle Alan closed the comicbook and handed it across to David who accepted it with all the reverence and respect that one might afford a priceless historical artifact. "Looks like a great story, David," he said. David nodded and turned the pages to that same part of the story where the man fell off the mountain. He placed his finger on one of the panels but, though for a second or so it seemed to take on a shimmering quality, it didn't actually move.

David looked up at his uncle in disappointment.

"Just a party trick, John," Uncle Alan was saying. Then he turned to David and gave a conspiratorial wink. "Maybe we'll check it out some more, huh?" he said softly, directing the question at David. "Maybe later?"

* * *

Thirty eight years later, driving along the section of derelict blacktop leading down into Forest Plains, David Milligan had seen that same expression... only this time it was on his wife's face, a silent and knowing wink, her right hand resting on his leg, squeezing it every now and again. If he had not seen that wink — that teasing *Guess what we're going to be doing when we finally get to Richard's house?* expression — maybe he would have seen the bend in the road.

And if he had seen Kathy unbuckling her seat strap, noticed her getting ready to snuggle up against him, put her head on his shoulder... maybe he would have told her to keep it fastened.

Then again, maybe he would have seen the tree.

Maybe, if he'd only glanced at the speedo, he would have noticed that he was going too fast, too fast for these winding roads.

But all he had seen was Kathy's eyes.

Running now, silently... always silently... everything so still and quiet... running along that same road carrying a piece of torn-out Oldsmobile dashboard with a strip of Scotch tape across it, running with the frozen-in-time countryside around him, hazy, like he was seeing it through gauze, David felt waves of guilt that were darker than he could bear to think about. If he had been concentrating on what he had been doing   namely driving the car, steering it along those winding roads — they would have been home now. Him and Kathy.

They would have been home and Kathy would not be lying half in and half out of the car, blood pooling from deep gashes in her neck, steam coming up from beneath the hood of the Olds, the car wrapped around the tree David hadn't seen.

Only now the blood wasn't pooling. And the steam wasn't rising. At least not for a little while. Thanks to the Scotch tape.

The first house came up on the left. David saw a

woman he recognized from other visits as Ellen Dworkin frozen in the act of taking sheets off the line, glancing up at a gathering gloom that would forever be caught at that single nanosecond of the gathering. It was only now that David realized that it must be windy out there... wherever 'out there' really was.

The sheet Ellen was removing stretched out in front of her and a thick hank of her hair had come free from her clasp sticking out at right angles to her head, while her dress was pinned tight to her backside, billowing around her knees but not moving.

Nothing was moving. At least, nothing David could see. But he could hear it. The distant rumbling that sounded like thunder over in the next county was not thunder. And it was a whole lot closer than the next county. He didn't have a lot of time.

David moved out around a flatbed truck he and Ellen had passed just a handful of real-time minutes ago, its driver — a gray-haired and -bearded man — caught in the act of singing... or so it appeared, his left hand holding the wheel as he negotiated the gentle bend that became Main Street and his right in the air like he was conducting an orchestra, eyes half-closed and his mouth twisted into a curious grimace, a waxen image from some bizarre mannequin display, lifelike but seemingly not life-filled. The scene was either a vacation snapshot taken by the worst photographer in the world or a badly-paused frame in a movie running on a VCR.

David switched the piece of dashboard to his other hand and fought off the urge to stop and take in the scene. The thunder sounded again, a little louder this time. There *was* a storm coming... though he knew that this particular weather-front had no foundation in meteorological fact.

He faced forward to the small town of Forest Plains and plowed into the silent stillness, gripping his dashboard and letting his mind drift back to the first time he had seen Bentley Grange and Uncle Alan.

* * *

"Is this *all* Uncle Alan's?" David asked, his forehead pressed against the car window as John Milligan drove past the twin concrete pillars leading up to Bentley Grange. It looked like the Ponderosa and David couldn't shake the idea that Pa Cartwright and his three sons were going to come riding over the ridge at any second, that jangly *dang daddleang daddleang daddleang daaddleaaaang daaaang!* music filling the still air all around them.

"Sure is," Dad said.

"Gee-ee-*ee!*" David exclaimed, stretching out the single syllable until it made three.

Eventually, the winding drive swooped down from the wooded hillside to become a graveled turning circle directly in front of the house. In the center of the circle a rustic concrete cherub perched in an oval dish of water, its mouth — the underlining in an expression which appeared to be as eroded from boredom as from the elements — served as the means (along with a little electricity, Dad explained) by which water was returned to the dish in which the cherub balanced in an endless stream of spit. Parked in front of the fountain, its right-hand pair of wheels well onto the grass, was a green Mustang convertible, its bodywork gleaming, its sandy-colored upholstery seeming to challenge someone to slide onto the seat, turn the key in the ignition and head out onto the endless highway.

Except for one thing: there *weren't* any endless highways in England and the few decent roads that did exist were not to be found in Wiltshire. Here, the mysterious and ancient Stonehenge held dominance over the gently undulating countryside and the road system — a complex series of winding veins and arteries — seemed forever in danger of colliding or, at best, overlapping.

The Milligans had been in England for a little over one week, having spent several days doing all the obligatory tourist things such as seeing the Tower of London, visiting the Houses of Parliament and the colossal Big Ben clocktower, and calling round at Buckingham Palace to see, according to David's father, the Queen.

David knew his father was an important man but this last revelation was something else entirely. So much so that, for the entire duration of their stay at the Royal Piccadilly Hotel, David had strutted around the carpeted corridors conveying his family's full importance to smiling men in striped vests and bustling ladies in black dresses overlaid with white aprons. They had all seemed suitably impressed.

Then David's father announced that they were going to visit mom's brother, Uncle Alan, who had just finished a long visit to somewhere called Tibet. Uncle Alan, Dad explained, was an adventurer of sorts and he had come back to England to re-charge his batteries.

Batteries? This early insight into the biological functions of the human anatomy caused David some concern on the journey to Wiltshire. Maybe this was why his mother had died so soon after Richard had appeared. Maybe *her* batteries had run down and she wasn't able to re-charge them in time. Come to think of it, David mused to himself sitting in the back seat of the car trying to ignore Richard's snoring, he didn't recall ever having his *own* batteries checked, never mind actually re-charged.

He looked down at his own body then, small legs sticking straight out over the seat edge, and wondered where these fabulous life-giving and life-preserving things could possibly be located. Then he fell asleep to the gentle motion of the car.

Bentley Grange was a big rambling two-story house set back from a lonely winding road in a small village called Ansty, mid-way between Salisbury and Shaftsbury. It was reached by a gravel drive that crunched noisily as they pulled onto it.

In fact, it was the noise that awoke David.

Richard was already awake, his eyes still sleepily lidded and his cheeks as red as over-ripe apples. He was trying to pull a thread from the large cushion in his lap, concentrating so intensely that he hadn't realized the car had pulled off the blacktop or that their destination was very close.

David stared in amazement.

The house spread before them, a seeming collection of extensions to the original property, replete with a profusion of leaded windows amidst the stonework, two tall chimneys — one of that was belching thick wafts of smoke which swirled themselves into a mixture of shapes both recognizable and strangely indistinct — and a small walkway, made out of a triptych of wood and glass, which led from the main house to a small outbuilding. This could have been designed to contain a car, David reckoned, but, with its two wide doors propped open, it was now a home to a collection of boxes of varying shapes and sizes, all stacked in piles haphazardly.

"Isn't there a garden?" David inquired.

"Round the back," came his father's reply.

David was out of the car and making for the side of the house even as John Milligan was turning off the ignition, and he could hear Richard's squeals of annoyance at being left behind. Ignoring his brother's protestations, David took in the landscape as he ran.

He had veered to the left where the land rose gently amidst small elderberry and apple trees to a rounded hill which effectively formed the horizon. Perched halfway up the hill was an old windmill, its wooden blades trailing colorful material, like scarves or flags, in the breeze. David came to a halt a little way from the building and considered heading across to explore but the consideration was short-lived. For a moment, the windmill looked like a disembodied arm protruding from the ground, its elongated fingers feeling sightlessly into the air, trailing the tattered garments of dead people it had passed on its way to the ground's surface.

That was one thing, and it was bad enough.

But what if the arm were *not* disembodied? What if it were still attached to a huge creature resting beneath grass and soil, a huge creature which might, at any moment, choose to sit upright, scattering everything around in sods and clumps of earth?

David felt a small shudder run down his back and he looked around to see what was happening back at the car.

Dad had Richard in his arms and he was talking to a man David had not seen before, though he assumed this was Uncle Alan. All three of them were standing watching David and when they saw him looking, Dad and Uncle Alan gave a short wave. David waved back and suddenly realized he needed to pee. He glanced alongside the house and saw that the garden at the back was huge. But even more than that, it was all chalk-marked as though ready for some kind of game though David had no idea what it might be. And sitting there was what looked to be a collection of statues some inside the chalk marks and some outside.

He could see a huge bird, its wings folded down. The bird seemed to be looking straight at him.

Behind the bird was a boy, young but older than David, and he was sitting on another bird, one with kind of a long beak... like the ones in the *Turok, Son Of Stone* comicbook that Danny Kobel had included in his generous pile, about a couple of Indians who kept on getting into battles with big dinosaurs some of which were bird-things with long scrawny beaks and huge wings — David's father had called them 'terrydackles'. David didn't like that comicbook at all.

In front of the bird-and-boy statue were a long-tailed fish, curled up and looking mighty lifelike — so lifelike that David half-expected it to move as he watched — and another couple of animal statues that David couldn't make out. He took a couple of steps alongside the house towards them and then stopped. Coming into view was some kind of cat-thing, sitting right in the middle of the chalked area, side-on to the house and staring straight ahead.

David frowned. These certainly were strange and wonderful statues. He took another step and then saw that the cat-thing had something in its mouth. It was a pipe.

"Hey, David?" David's father shouted. "Come and say hello to Uncle Alan."

David span around and, as he started to run back, he remembered that he needed to go to the bathroom. He hoped the movement might prevent him from wetting himself.

* * *

David Milligan, aged 43, knew he must be exerting himself. He knew he should be panting breathlessly — though he felt fine and not at all stretched physically stretched — and that his feet must be making contact with the ground but there was no sound.

As he ran up to the intersection of Main and Sycamore he stopped, placed the dashboard under his arm and felt for his pulse. He was a little dismayed to discover that he couldn't find it.

Maybe he was dead.

Maybe the shock of the accident had caused his heart to stop or the accident itself had taken its toll on him too.

Maybe all of this was simply a moment-of-death hallucination, a corpse's dream of regret for allowing all he held so dear to slip through his fingers.

Maybe, right now, he was sitting back in the Olds, smiling a bloody rictus grin through the shattered windshield, staring forever at his wife's backside while the front of her lay on the hood... with the steering wheel crushed into his rib cage and his Fruit Of The Looms filled with fresh manure.

A hollow rumble that seemed to shake the air sounded behind him. David glanced back as he turned into Sycamore Street, slowing down a little.

The street shimmered as though he were looking

Lonesome Roads

through a heat haze, the sun causing the blacktop to overheat. But it was late afternoon / early evening. It had been late afternoon / early evening when he had wrecked the car and it would be late afternoon / early evening for evermore... or at least until the storm broke. There was no way of riding it out.

He removed the dashboard from beneath his arm, turned back and ran on. Not far now. He could see the MD sign a little way up the street.

* * *

Uncle Alan had organized a great supper for them on that long-ago first day of their stay at Bentley Grange... except he had called it 'afternoon tea'.

A huge trestle table was laid out on the back lawn alongside a paved path leading from the back door. Plates of sandwiches — daintily cut from slices of bread and filled with cold meats — rubbed shoulders with dishes of salad, tomatoes and Uncle Alan's homemade coleslaw. At the end of the feast, stuffed to bursting with food and 7Up and lemonade, David watched warily as the shadows lengthened and bedtime drew near.

Richard had already gone down, exhausted from staggering around on the grass all afternoon and playing with the statues, and David had watched in fascination as his father and Uncle Alan had stood at the door of his kid brother's room, listening to their whispered conversation from his vantage point at the head of the stairs.

"He's quite a boy," Uncle Alan had said, resting a hand on John Milligan's shoulder. "They both are."

David's father nodded without looking around. "They are that."

"Look like their mother, too."

"You think so?"

"No question of it. Just look at that mouth and nose. Seems to me like she's living again through her kids."

David's father hadn't said anything to that. He had just kept on watching.

"You miss her, huh?"

"Alan, you just wouldn't believe."

Uncle Alan had nodded and let out a big sigh. "She misses you too, John," he had said, squeezing David's father's shoulder as they both turned away from the bedroom and pulled the door slowly closed. David had slid back until he was out of sight and had then ran down the stairs and back outside, his mind ablaze with wonder. It hadn't been so much at what his uncle had said but at the calm certainty and conviction with which he had said it.

But that was a couple of hours ago.

Now the day looked almost done for David too, and he stifled a yawn so as not to bring the dreaded moment any closer.

"You tired, big guy?" Uncle Alan asked. He was standing by the trestle table clearing away the remains of the meal, moving plates festooned with fatty rinds of ham, beef and chicken, pieces of tomato stalk, crumbs and swirls of coleslaw.

"Uh uh." David shook his head. "Where's my dad?"

"Upstairs." Uncle Alan balanced plates and cups and glasses precariously on the big tray and looked around for things he'd missed. "Taking a rest, I think. He's tired, I guess."

"*I'm* not tired," David said, matter-of-factly.

"You sure?"

"I wanna play catch some more. You wanna play catch with me?"

Uncle Alan frowned and looked up at the sky. "Be dark soon. Won't be able to see to catch."

"Not dark yet, though," David said, annoyed with himself that he had been unable to keep the whine out of his voice. He sounded like a girl. "Dad says I don't have to go to bed until the sun goes down." He pointed to the red disk shimmering in the sky way back behind the rooftop and chimneys of Bentley Grange. "It's a ways off yet."

Uncle Alan looked at him for what seemed like an

eternity. Then he set the tray of plates back on the table and said, "You want to stay up a while, huh?"

David nodded but scowled. "Dad says only till sundown though. And I promised him. Whether he's around or not."

"Yeah, well, maybe we can do something about that."

"You gonna talk to my dad? Gee, that'd be-"

"Nope, I'm not going to talk to your dad. Your dad needs some rest, David. I'm going to make it so's you can stay up a while longer — not a whole lot, mind, but a little while — without you having to go back on your word."

David swung a foot and kicked at the table leg. "How you gonna do that?" he asked. He didn't sound hopeful.

"Why, I'm going to delay sundown!" And with that, he turned around and walked into the house.

* * *

David stopped on the sidewalk and placed a hand on the picket fence surrounding the lawn of the MD's house. It felt like sponge. He pulled his hand away and looked up at the sign.

Richard K A Milligan, MD

He reached down for the catch on the gate but it too felt like it was made out of something porous, like it was only partly finished. No matter how he tried, David could not make the catch move or the gate open.

Another crack of thunder sounded on the outskirts of town, gigantic trashcans being rolled down some celestial alleyway and bouncing against the walls all the way.

David looked around to see if he could see anything but there was nothing. Everything seemed completely normal, like a photograph of any small-town street at the close of the day.

Halfway along, a couple of cars were either pulling out from places diagonal to the sidewalk or pulling into them. The people in the cars were caught in the act of speaking, of looking over shoulders if they were reversing or checking cross-traffic, leaning forward to see around their passengers, checking the road.

On the sidewalk across the road, two young boys slouched forever towards a distant adolescent Babylon, mouths twisted and curled around words that they were caught in the middle of, experiences and conquests only partly revealed, one boy's foot frozen only inches from a large round rock lying in the middle of the paving slabs. Above them, branches curled backwards in a wind that David could not see and could not feel.

In the house next door to Richard's a man in a gaudily-striped shirt stood in the center of his garden, a hose in one hand and his other hand thrust deep into his pocket. The stream of water remained caught in time, one end still attached to the hose while the other end, all fanned out into a fine spray, had just settled that very nanosecond onto petal and leaf while the drops immediately behind had been halted in mid-flight.

David stepped over the gate and walked up the path. As he got closer to the screen door he noticed a hand holding onto the curtain of the window which looked out of a room somewhere alongside the door and out onto the road. He stepped onto the grass and leaned over, though the secrecy with which he did it was completely unnecessary. Whoever owned the hand would not be able to see him.

The person who owned the hand was Richard, his face staring out onto the late afternoon street, frowning, wondering where Big Brother had got to... concerned because maybe something was spoiling in the kitchen.

David moved further across and saw Margaret standing behind Richard. She was smoking a cigarette, her head tilted back, her eyes half closed and her mouth partly open in that split second when she was blowing smoke out, blowing it up into the air the way Margaret always did when she was in company and didn't want to blow it over anyone else.

David lifted the piece of dashboard, took a deep breath and pulled off the Scotch tape.

Suddenly everything started moving again.

Margaret blew out her smoke. Somewhere behind David, conversations recommenced, a man watered his garden, Ellen Dworkin gathered her washing and a boy kicked a stone. David heard the stone skittering along the sidewalk, heard the wind rustling the trees, heard a car horn *blaaat!* and a dog howl. But he did not hear any thunder.

He waved madly as Richard was letting the curtain fall back into place.

"Jesus Christ!" Richard mouthed. "They're here."

"Here! Where?" David could hear Margaret's voice even through all the double glazing on the windows. Her face appeared next to Richard's. She too was frowning. Richard moved out of sight and David pulled the roll of Scotch tape out of his pocket as he moved back to the path to greet his kid brother.

"Where the holy hell did you spring-"

While Richard was speaking, his arms open wide in welcome, the inner door continuing to open as he held the screen door ajar with his foot, David lurched across the grass, a torn strip of tape in one hand and the piece of Oldsmobile dashboard in the other.

"David?" Richard said.

"Where's my favorite brother in law?" Margaret was saying in a high excited voice, probably playing for time while she stubbed out her cigarette. "And where's Katherine?"

David threw an arm around his kid brother and pulled him out onto the grass. The sun seemed to have dropped miles in the few seconds since David had removed the first piece of tape. And he knew that, back at the Oldsmobile, the steam was once more rising from the buckled hood... and Kathy's blood was flowing again, flowing hard and fast around the pieces of glass in her neck.

The two of them fell to their knees and Richard was half laughing and half annoyed, saying to David, "What the hell are you *doing*, Dave?" while David placed the piece of dashboard right on the shadow of sunlight on the lawn, the shadow cast by David's small outhouse where they kept the garden tools. With his arm around Richard's neck, David placed the piece of tape so that it straddled the shadow on the dashboard, one half of the tape on the shadow itself and the other half on the piece of dashboard with the sun's full light shining down on it.

All sound stopped.

David closed his eyes and bit on his lip, hardly daring to move, waiting to feel his brother turn into some kind of useless sponge beneath his arm.

"Okay, okay," said Richard, who was having to fight hard to keep from falling over entirely, "you wanna tell me... you wanna tell me-"

David kept his eyes closed.

"Dave?" Richard Milligan's voice sounded a little hoarse suddenly.

David closed his eyes tighter.

"Dave, what the hell is going on here? Everything has stopped moving."

David rolled onto his side and looked around. It was true. Across the street the man in the gaudily-striped shirt was caught in the act of placing his hose on the grass and maybe coming across to see what was going on. Either that or maybe going back inside to call for the police because Doctor Milligan was fighting on his front lawn with some kind of vagrant.

On the sidewalk a little way up the street, the two boys were still kicking stones except now one of them had his arm stretched out, fist clenched, about to punch his friend in the shoulder.

"Oh, God, *Margaret!*"

David span looked to the side and saw his brother getting to his feet, staring back at the house. When he looked back he saw the strangest sight: Margaret Milligan was frozen in the act of running down the path, caught mid-step between two rows of small rose trees, her elbows crooked, her arms looking like piston rods on some old steam train... and the image was completed by Margaret's head thrown back and her mouth rounded into a perfect 'O' as she puffed out the last vestiges of cigarette smoke.

"Leave her, Rich," David said. But it was too late.

Richard ran up to his wife and threw his arms about her, whispering to her. It was the strangest sight. Strange because, despite the momentum with which Richard greeted his wife and which he then employed in terms of sheer energy to hold her and attempt to console her... despite all that, Margaret did not appear to move so much as the tiniest fraction of an inch. There was no sign of shaking or instability. She was just solid.

Richard stepped back from her, his hands still on her shoulders.

"Rich," David said, "we have to talk."

Richard turned around, still holding onto his wife. "You know something about this?" He waved an arm around him.

Before David could answer, a roll of thunder rattled from south of town and boomed over their heads so hard that David and Richard could feel their eyeballs rattle in their sockets.

"What the-" Richard began. "And now we get a storm?"

David shook his head. "It's not a storm."

David's brother frowned. "So what is it?"

"It's the monitor," David said. And he began to explain.

* * *

While David had spent time wandering around the statues in the garden of Bentley Grange, Uncle Alan had been going around the perimeter of the lawn re-chalking over the chalk-lines with what looked like a piece of granite.

David was standing beside a statue of a girl in a flowing dress perched on one leg. She was a ballerina, Uncle

Alan had told them during their meal.

And behind her was another girl, this time in a bathing costume, sitting astride some kind of big-footed lizard thing. She was holding a tennis raquet.

"What are all these things for, Uncle Alan?" David had asked.

"Let's say they came with the house," Uncle Alan had said. He'd replied in the same tone of voice that David's father used when he didn't want to get into a conversation.

David ran across to the big cat-thing with the pipe and tried to clamber onto its back. After a couple of failed attempts, he flopped down onto the grass beside it and watched his uncle.

"Whatcha doing, Uncle Alan?" David asked.

"Oh, just making sure we keep safe," came the reply.

David watched his uncle go around the entire perimeter of the garden re-chalking the lines that already existed.

"Are we gonna play a game?"

"Kind of," said Uncle Alan.

"We gonna play catch?"

"Nope."

David walked over to where his uncle was chalking and studied his work carefully. "Doesn't look like a baseball dimc-ond."

"It isn't." Uncle Alan reached the end, a position marked with an old roll of Scotch tape lying in the grass, and he stood up dusting his hands against his trousers. There was no chalk left.

"We gonna play now?" David asked, "Before the sun goes down?"

Uncle David laughed. "Don't worry, big guy... the sun won't be going down and spoiling *this* game."

David frowned. He looked around for the ball and bats they had been playing with earlier, after Richard had finally gone to bed, but someone had cleared them away.

113

Lonesome Roads

He was about to inquire just how they were going to play this very unusual game when Uncle Alan crouched down beside him and took hold of his shoulders.

"David."

"Sir?"

"David, we're going to play a game... kind of a show... like the circus?"

David nodded. He knew what a circus was. He'd seen *Circus Boy* on the TV so he knew what a circus was just fine.

"But I want you to do everything I say. Can you promise me you'll do that for me?"

David nodded emphatically. "Sure," he said, the way he had heard his father speak on the telephone. Assured and confident. Heck, he would promise anything right now just so's they could get on with the game.

"Okay." Uncle Alan sat back on the grass right next to the shadow of the house, stretching towards David as the sun gradually settled itself in the distant clouds behind the house. He lifted the old roll of Scotch tape and pulled the end free. When he had pulled off about a foot of the stuff he lifted the roll to his mouth and bit a tiny chip into the side, then tore off the strip.

"Whatcha doing with the tape?"

"Shh!" Uncle Alan said. "Just watch."

David's uncle carefully placed the tape so that it ran across the shadow made by the setting sun, sticking the two ends down onto the grass as best as he could. Then he moved slowly away from it and looked up into the sky. And he smiled. "Never fails to amaze me," he said.

David followed his uncle's gaze and saw, directly overhead, a pair of birds motionless against the clouds. The clouds themselves had a faintly orange and purple hue and one of the birds had been frozen in mid swoop, its wings trailing out alongside. It looked like a woman diving out of the sky.

"Hey," David said. "They're not moving!"

"That's right," said Uncle Alan. He lowered his head and pointed to the field beyond the garden where a horse was standing, its neck arched and its mane thrown out like the tassels on Davy Crokett's jacket sleeves.

"The horse isn't moving neither," said David.

"Either," Uncle Alan corrected him.

"Mmm," said David. "Either." He looked around and was suddenly aware that all sound had stopped apart from their two voices. Getting to his feet, he said, "I'm gonna go stroke it."

Uncle Alan's hand shot out like a fisherman's net and grabbed David's arm. "No, you must *not* leave the protected area." He pointed. "See the chalk marks?"

A roll of distant thunder sounded somewhere way out in front of them. "Why not?" David asked, startled by the sound.

"It's not safe."

"Why isn't it safe? There's nothing there."

Uncle Alan nodded his head. "There's something there but you just can't see it. It can see you, though.

"It walks around the land between the lines like an actor prowling the stage behind the theatrical curtain which separates the play from the audience," he said. The words didn't make much sense to David. "All it's looking for," Uncle Alan added, "is a way through the curtain."

David shuddered. He glanced back at the house, saw the windows, still and silent, devoid of life. They were the same windows as they had been before Uncle Alan had laid the tape but now they looked different somehow. Another roll of thunder boomed, this time a little louder.

"Where's my dad?"

"He's in bed, asleep. He needs his rest, big guy." David's uncle turned to him and smiled a sad smile. "It's been a difficult time for your dad."

David nodded. "He misses mom, I guess."

"Yes he does."

"I miss mom, too," David said. It was true. He hadn't

Lonesome Roads

actually realized before just how much he did miss her, and for the first real time in almost two years he was aware that he wouldn't see her again. His chin started to shake and he bit onto his bottom lip in an attempt to stop the tears... but they were well on their way.

"Let it come," Uncle Alan said. "Crying's good for the soul like rain's good for the garden. Cleans it up, makes it fresh." He leaned his back against the cat-thing statue and reached and put his arm around David. David snuggled into his uncle's shoulder, feeling the tears make the shirt wet beneath his face.

"Sounds like... sounds like we're going to get a lot of rain for the garden," David said, recalling his father's favorite phrase every time a storm broke back home. He spoke into the material, his voice muffled and his breath warm and reassuring. He felt sleepy suddenly.

"Could be," Uncle Alan said, but he didn't sound convinced. Rather his voice had a faint tinge of nervousness mixed with excitement, insistent but hesitant, its sound pulling David into sleep.

They sat like that for a while, David resting his head and Uncle Alan watching in all directions. The thunder got louder and more frequent, and David awoke with a start.

"Thunder's getting louder," David said.

Uncle Alan nodded.

"How'd you make everything stop?" David asked, shuffling around so that he could look at the horse. It hadn't moved.

"The tape."

"Is it magic?"

"I guess you could call it magic, yes."

"Where'd you get it?"

"Oh," Uncle Alan's voice became wistful. "A long ways from here. There are lots of magic things out there if you've got the patience and you know where to look."

David thought about that for a minute and a big crack of thunder made him jump. It sounded like it had ripped the sky apart and David half expected to look up and see a huge tear in the clouds, like the one in his jeans, with darkness spilling out of it and tumbling to the Earth in a spray of stars and comets and meteors.

"Uncle Alan?"

"Yes?"

"That thunder... it isn't *real* thunder is it?"

"No, it's not real thunder."

"What is it?"

"It's the Monitor."

David sat up quickly. "The man eater?"

Uncle Alan laughed. "The *Monitor*."

"What's a monitor?"

"A monitor is someone who listens."

David frowned. "Then why isn't he a listener?"

"Because a monitor does something about what it hears."

David looked across the fields. The clouds had not moved but the distant hills looked darker, hazy somehow. "And what does the monitor hear?"

"It hears us."

"Why? We're not doing anything."

"We're in its domain. It hears our presence."

David scratched his backside and shuffled himself into a more comfortable position. "What's a domain?"

"A land... a world."

"But we're just in *our* world. Aren't we?"

"Well, yes and no." Uncle Alan shifted his weight from his left arm to his right arm, flexing the fingers on his left and grimacing at the pins and needles feeling in their tips. "You remember what I told you? About the comicbook story you showed me?"

"'The Hand From Beyond'?"

"That's the one."

David tried to whistle and it came out like air from a busted radiator. "That's a neat story."

Uncle Alan said, "It sure is," but his words were

117

Lonesome Roads

drowned out by a roll of thunder so loud and so long that David thought his head was going to explode.

"I'm frightened."

"Don't be. We're safe so long as we stay inside the markings."

"What does the man-eater want?"

"It wants to find out what we're doing in its land." Uncle Alan pushed David upright and flexed his other hand.

"This is the man-eater's land?"

"Kind of." Uncle David stood up and stretched. "This is the space between the lines, David. The tiniest fragment in time when everything is in flux and nothing is decided. Everything is to play for... but you must move fast." He pointed out towards the fields without saying anything.

David looked.

The land a few hundred yards in front of them dropped away sharply onto a long, wide plain that stretched into the distance. Way way away, where the hills met the sky, the air seemed to be shimmering, growing darker and somehow less distinct.

It was as though the entire sky was indeed a flattened curtain, with all the clouds drawn on it; and now it did look as though someone or something were behind that curtain, struggling to find a way through.

"Here it comes," Uncle Alan whispered.

* * *

David and his brother were still in the garden in Forest Plains, Richard's wife standing like a waxwork on the path and David holding a broken piece of car dashboard like it was some kind of holy grail.

"Rich listen to me."

"I'm listening."

David took hold of his younger brother's shoulders and shook them once, gently but firmly. "You have to listen," he said, "and you have not to interrupt. Do you understand?"

Richard glanced across at his wife, frozen in mid-step, blowing smoke like a train, smoke frozen into a small opaque cloud over her head and partly obscuring her mouth like a veil. "No, I don't understand any of it."

"Well, maybe we'll have time for questions when we're done."

"When we're *done*? When we're done with *what*?"

"Richard, just listen."

Richard listened.

"You remember Uncle Alan?"

Richard shook his head. "I remember hearing about him from somewhere. Mom's brother or Dad's?"

"Mom's."

"Did I ever meet him?"

David nodded. "Mom hadn't been dead long. We went to England to stay with him at a place called Bentley Grange. I guess it was just for Dad to get his head into some kind of gear. I was six years old or so, so you would be around two." David looked down at the piece of dashboard.

"One night after you'd gone to bed — Dad had gone, too: he was bushed — Uncle Alan... he did this thing. I thought it was like a trick."

"A trick?"

"He froze time for everything and everyone except him and me. He did it by placing a piece of Scotch tape across the shadow cast by the setting sun and somehow — don't ask me how — this stopped the sun from setting any more." He ran quickly through the events from that fateful night.

"'Everything is to play for'? 'You must move fast'?" Richard wanted to laugh at the garbled story outline that his brother had told him but somehow, with everything that had happened, he couldn't raise so much as a smile. "Sounds like something out of Carlos Casteneda or 'Zen And The Art Of Weather Forecasting'."

"Rich, believe me, we don't have the time. Kathy needs your help."

"Hey, where *is* Kathy?"

"I'll get to that. You have to hear the rest first."

"You've hypnotized me, right?" Richard took hold of his head with both hands and moved it from side to side, his eyes firmly closed. "Power of suggestion. And when I open my eyes..."

Richard opened his eyes and looked around. Nothing had changed.

"So Uncle Alan froze time for everyone but him and me," David continued, "and we sat waiting for the Monitor."

"Which is?" Richard asked as he walked across to Margaret.

David shrugged. "I don't know. I only know it's big and it gets pissed off when you do the Scotch tape thing. Seems there's a way you can keep safe but that's only by chalking lines around yourself." He smiled but it was a smile without any humor. "We don't have any of that particular chalk."

"But you've got the tape?"

David patted the bulge in his pocket. "I've got the tape."

Richard was trying to open Margaret's lips with his finger but he wasn't having any success. "Feels strange," he said as he removed his finger and looked first at it and then at his wife's mouth. "Her skin."

"'Unfinished' is the way I describe it. Almost completed but not quite." He walked over to his brother and rested a hand on his shoulder. "Rich, we really do have to move."

Thunder rolled somewhere off Sycamore and down Main Street, sounding like someone drumming on a sheet of thin pressed metal, echoing and reverberating.

Richard turned and looked up into the sky, expecting maybe to see some lightning. But there was nothing to see and, apart from the slowly disappearing aural ripples of the thunder, nothing at all to hear.

"That the Monitor?" Richard asked. "Doing a kind of 'fee fi fo fum' routine?"

David nodded, pulling Richard towards the front door. "That's about it."

"Look, if I buy this — and I haven't yet said that I do, at least not totally — what does it look like?"

"The Monitor?"

Richard nodded.

"I don't know."

Inside the house, Richard asked, "How come you don't know what it looks like, this monitor thing, when it came to you and Uncle Alan?"

"I got scared."

"And what happened?"

* * *

The sky in front of them shimmered and warped, shot through now with colored flashes which stayed for a moment and then merged into each other, running like paints on a palette, creating new hues and shades, each one then fading away like a spent firecracker flash. But shooting through it all now was a darkness, many shades of black and gray, swirling in thick clouds of intensity, roiling like flood waters coursing over rocks.

A wind seemed to have come up.

David could hear it. He could feel it blowing against his face from the dark clouds.

"Is this it?" David shouted into the wind as he turned to look at Uncle Alan. "Is this the man-eater?"

Uncle Alan's hair was blowing back from his head. He kept on staring forward. David had seen that kind of intensity before.

He had seen it on a handful of the faces that regularly dotted the congregation at the little church back in Cedar Rapids, faces that seemed to shine with a fervor of belief and expectation... and maybe just a little fear.

"Here it comes," Uncle Alan said, his voice little more than a whisper.

David turned and looked.

Now an entire column of sky in front of them was pulsating, pushing forward towards David and his uncle and making everything behind it seem as though they were looking at it through the curvature of a glass bottle.

David craned his neck so far back that he was almost staring straight up into space, and yet still the column stretched and bulged... like a curtain that concealed something trying to get out.

Sure enough, the 'curtain' started to tear.

"I'm frightened," David said.

Without turning away from the scene in front of them, Uncle Alan said, "Don't be. It can't get at us because I've re-chalked the boundaries."

David glanced down at the chalkline around where they were sitting and then looked up at the funnel of energy.

The sky had split open, a darkness behind it spilling out like gas, slowly swirling forward and gathering itself into some kind of shape. The split carried on lengthening, slowly widening as it grew longer, the blackness pouring out faster and faster, the shape pulling together quicker.

Thunder sounded right above them.

The wind blew stronger, straight at them out of the rip in the sky, and Uncle Alan said something but David couldn't hear what it was. He watched as his uncle got first to his knees and then started to stand, faltering in the face of the wind. He was smiling.

David looked back at the split and saw that it now stretched down from high, high in the sky almost all the way to the ground on the plain below them. Everywhere was growing dark.

"I'm *frightened*!" David said again but his words were lost in the sound of the wind. He snuggled into the cold side of the pipe-smoking cat-thing and tried to get away from the wind and the tearing sky.

He looked around to make sure that there was nobody — or, more importantly, n*othing*! — creeping up behind them and saw the tape still on the grass, its edges curling up from the tufts of green.

David jumped to his feet and turned his back on the gathering blackness.

Uncle Alan saw him and turned, his face frowning with puzzlement but still smiling. David saw his uncle's lips move but heard nothing but the wind. As he ran across to the tape he felt his legs almost running away with him, making his move so quickly that, for a second, he feared that he was going to run right past it and out over the chalklines... feared that the statues were going to come to life and stop him... that the pipe-smoking cat-thing was going to drop that pipe and try something else in its sadly smiling mouth.

"David!"

He heard his uncle's voice now, crying out in panic. But it was too late.

David threw himself down onto the ground, almost rolling over the tape. His hand shot out and grabbed a corner. He pulled it up as he continued to roll and felt it come completely into his hand.

Everything went silent.

Then it wasn't.

The sounds of the late evening had returned. Insects were going about their business and, from somewhere way away, David heard the sounds of a car engine traveling the distant roads. He looked down into his hand and saw the crumpled Scotch tape.

"Why?" his uncle said from behind him.

"I was frightened the man-eater was going to get us," David explained.

Now that the blackness had gone and the sky was no longer ripped, David felt a little foolish. He waited to see if his uncle was going to shout at him. Maybe he was even going to tell David's father.

Uncle Alan plopped onto the grass next to David.

"We would have been safe," he said. "I thought you might like to see it."

"Have you seen it?"

Uncle Alan shook his head. "I've been waiting for the right time." He picked up the roll of Scotch tape and tore off another strip which he wound around his wrist. Then he offered the roll to David. David accepted it, looked at it and then looked at his uncle.

"There isn't much tape left on there," Uncle Alan said. "Only a few strips by my reckoning. I want you to keep it."

David frowned. "Why?"

"Because one day you might need it."

"Why might I need the man-eater?"

Uncle Alan laughed and rested on his elbows. "You won't need the Monitor but you might need to hold things up for a while. But there isn't any more chalk. I used the last bit on this." He waved an arm at the chalklines around where they sat. "So if you do ever use it, you won't have any protection."

"I want to go to bed," David said.

"Okay." Uncle Alan started to get up. "You want me to come up and tuck you in?"

David shook his head. "Uh uh. I can do it myself."

"Okay."

"You coming in yet?"

"No, I think I'm just going to sit a while and catch the end of the day."

There was something about the way Uncle Alan said that, something that, down the years, David would wonder if he had noticed at the time or that he had picked up as he had gotten older, replaying the scene over and over again in his mind.

Less than a half-hour later, after he had looked in on his father who seemed to be sleeping so deeply that he hadn't the heart to disturb him, David crept quietly into the room he shared with Richard and went straight to the window.

Outside, it was darker than it had been when he left the garden. But it still wasn't so dark that he could not the still and silent statues or his uncle sitting on the grass overlooking the plain. David shuffled a chair across to the window so that he could stand on it and see what his uncle was doing.

Uncle Alan was outside the chalklines. There was something about this sudden realization that made David feel nervous.

The sun's light had moved the shadow of Bentley Grange closer and closer to edge of the field, completely filling in the area that David had first thought was some kind of games pitch.

He watched as Uncle Alan pulled the tape from his wrist and prepared to lay it carefully across the last tiny sliver of sunlight between the shadows.

David started to shout as his uncle placed the tape on the grass and, for a brief instant, Uncle Alan looked up at David's window and smiled.

But he continued to place the tape.

Then, as soon as it was in position, Uncle Alan was gone.

And there was no longer any sign of the piece of tape.

* * *

"He'd left a note in the kitchen," David said, finishing the story. "I ran in and woke Dad and we went downstairs and there it was, propped up against a bowl of flowers. I'll remember that bowl of flowers as long as I live."

"What did it say?"

David shrugged. "I don't remember the exact words. Dad read it aloud and then put the note in his pocket. Something about Uncle Alan having to go away and that he didn't know when he'd be back."

"I take it he never came back?"

"Not as far as I know." David walked across to the window and looked out.

"I take it you believe he laid the tape and time stopped," Richard said. "And in that stopped time, when he was moving and you weren't, the Monitor came for him... took the tape, too?"

"I suppose so, yes. What other explanation could there be?"

"And what do you think it did — did to *him* — when it got him?"

"I have absolutely no idea." David leaned forward so that his face was almost against the window and looked up into the sky. "It's starting to get dark," he said. "Look."

Richard joined him. They could hear the soft moaning of wind.

"Okay," Richard said. "I'm sold. So tell me about Kathy."

"We had an accident." David turned away from the window. "Kathy went through the windshield."

"How bad?"

"I don't know. She was breathing but there was a lot of blood. Pieces of glass in her neck." He shook his head and placed his free hand on the table for support.

"And you just *happened* to have the tape?"

"I've *always* had it. Carried it everywhere. To school and later to college with my books, to the office in my briefcase and at all other times it's been in the trunk of the car."

"You've had a lot of cars, Dave. The tape was in every one?"

David nodded. "I became quite intense about it. Pathetic really."

"Didn't turn out that way," Richard said. "And, if it's any consolation, I never noticed you carrying the thing around."

"I was very careful — probably because I didn't have any good idea as to why I was doing it. In fact, this past few years I've more or less forgotten about it. But when we had the accident..."

"Let me see it."

David pulled the roll of tape from his pocket. It looked just like any other roll of Scotch tape... except for the fact that there was hardly any tape left on the spool.

"There's not much," Richard said, his tone sounding negative.

"No, and we're going to need all of it.

"First off, I'm going to have to take off the piece that's on the dashboard to allow you time to get everything you need. Then we're going to have to get out to your car and, with me holding onto you and your..."

"Stuff," Richard offered.

"Your stuff," David continued, "and your car. That way we'll all be able to move when I place another piece on the dashboard."

"Jesus Christ." Richard let out a long sigh. "And what about this Monitor thing?"

David gave a small ironic smile. "It'll follow us."

"And when it gets us?"

"Let's not think about that."

"Okay," Richard said.

David followed his brother into a small office, the walls of which were lined with shelves, each one containing various equipment and bottles.

Richard looked at the shelves, muttering to himself. Then he turned to David and said, "I suppose we'd better get started."

David pulled off the tape.

"Okay, sterile gauze dressing packs," Richard said, pulling two packs from the shelf to his right. "IV line and fluids... saline, plasma expander..." He lifted a box from the next shelf down and another packet from the desktop behind him.

"Richard?" Margaret's voice boomed from outside. "Richard, where *are* you?"

Richard lifted a plastic-covered kit from a drawer in the large cabinet behind the door. "Tracheotomy kit, en-

Lonesome Roads

dotracheal tubes..." More packets and boxes went into the basket that Richard had given to David. "Drugs... let's see: we'll need adrenaline, steroids, syringes — mustn't forget the godamn syringes." The packets went into the basket just as Margaret appeared at the room door.

"Richard? What are you doing?" She frowned and scratched her head. "I was right behind you and then... and then you weren't there." She seemed to see David then and smiled.

"Hi Dave." She gave him a kiss on the cheek and hugged him close. David could smell cigarette smoke. It smelled good, normal.

"Hi Mags," David said around a weak smile.

"Hey," Margaret said, looking behind the door. "Where's Kath?"

"No time to talk, hon," Richard said.

Margaret watched her husband loading things into the basket. "What are you doing?"

Richard turned around and lifted the basket.

"That it?" David asked.

Richard nodded.

"Then let's go."

They brushed past Margaret and ran outside. Margaret followed.

Out on the street everything was normal again. People were walking, cars were moving by... and the sun was getting lower in the sky.

And somewhere on the outskirts of town, David's wife was once again bleeding to death. Maybe even already dead. David refused to consider that possibility.

"Where's your car?"

"Garage," Richard hissed.

"You'll have to get it out and bring it up to here." David pointed to the ground where the shadow cast by the buildings across the street was lengthening towards the house wall.

"Will somebody tell me that the hell's going on?"

Margaret snapped as her husband ran to the garage, jingling his car keys. "And what exactly is *that*?" she asked, pointing to the piece of dashboard in David's hand.

Before David could tell her that they didn't have the time to explain, Richard's Toyota was up alongside him, the door swinging open.

"Okay." David placed the piece of dashboard on the ground, right where the light gave way to shadow, and pulled a small piece of tape from a roll he produced from his pocket.

"Rich-*ard*," Margaret said in a sing-song voice, "I don't *like* this."

David placed one arm around Richard — a basket jammed full of medical supplies swinging from the middle of it — and then looked at the ground.

"It's no good," David said and Margaret watched as he hung his head. "I can't hold everything *and* get the tape in place."

"Maybe it'll still work if I hold the car and the basket and you," Richard ventured, "and that'll give you both hands free to get the tape in place."

David nodded.

A few seconds later they had shuffled around so that Richard now held the basket in the crook of his right arm — the hand of which held onto the door of the Toyota — while his left hand was locked firmly on the back of David's neck. David meanwhile had crouched down and was now placing the piece of tape he had removed from the roll onto what looked to Margaret like a battered piece of car dashboard.

"Richard, if somebody does not tell me what's goi-"

The tape was in place.

David looked up and saw Margaret leaning over him, her finger pointing out straight from a clenched fist. Without turning around, David said, "Rich? You still there?"

Richard removed his hand from David's neck and slid into the car, cursing as he hit his leg on the basket.

129

"Wait until I give you the nod and then pull off the tape. I'm going to do a couple of things that you'd probably be better off not seeing."

"Like what?"

"I'm going to fix her up to an IV drip for starters — saline and plasma expander to keep up her blood volume — then I'm going to check down her throat to see just how much damage has been done, maybe intubate her with an endotracheal tube to allow sufficient ventilation and I'm also going to inject her with adrenaline and steroids. And I'm going to place a pressure dressing on the wounds... the kind of thing they use in *MASH*? That should enable us to get her into hospital without her bleeding to death."

"That's if she's alive to start off with," David ventured.

"That's if she's alive to start off with."

David looked back along the road.

The funnel was ripping open and black gas was swirling out into the air, already forming a shape.

The gas — or whatever it was — had pooled down to the ground about fifty yards away, making long thick tendrils that squatted on either side of the road. Above the tendrils was a huge circular mass onto which more gas was attaching itself. In the rip behind it, David could see only stars and swirling shapes that looked like galaxies in a science fiction movie.

"Doesn't look good," David said.

"It'll be fine. Take off the tape and we're home and dry."

David lifted the piece of dashboard and took hold of the tape. *Yes*, he thought, *but when we put it on again, that thing's going to be there waiting for us when we have to drive through it.* He pulled the tape clear.

The Oldsmobile hissed and steam bellowed from the crushed hood.

David looked back along the road. The funnel was gone.

"Okay," Richard said, "you go and look the other way. And Dave..."

"Yeah?"

"There's another road into town. It's not a freeway exactly but it means we don't have to drive through the beastie, okay?"

David nodded and smiled, though he wasn't sure whether that would be much of an advantage.

* * *

Fifteen minutes later, Richard announced he was finished.

The good news — which Richard had delivered in the first few seconds after David had removed the tape — had been that Kathy was indeed alive and that things were not as bad as they had looked. But she would certainly have died if David had not had the Scotch tape.

She had severed her jugular but as luck would have it the offending piece of windshield had blocked most of the hole it had made doing the job in the first place. She had a bad lump on her head and her face was badly cut. Concussion was to be expected. Richard had found evidence of broken ribs — though no signs of internal bleeding — plus a broken shoulder and collarbone. All of this was fixable, Richard had explained to his brother in a gently reassuring voice.

David looked around and prepared himself.

Kathy was now on the ground and Richard had cleaned up most of the blood from her face. A huge plaster was fixed to her neck and Richard was holding some kind of bottle containing a clear fluid with a flexible pipe that traveled all the way to Kathy's wrist where it disappeared beneath a tight-looking bandage. David was pleased to see his wife's chest moving up and down, albeit slowly and with some apparent difficulty.

"Okay," Richard said, "Time to go time."

David shook his head. "You're going to have to-"

"Okay: here's what we do.

"We put Kathy in the back of the Toyota, still in real

Lonesome Roads

time, then you hold onto me and the car and do your tape thing on the dashboard. With any luck," Richard said, cautiously holding a single finger aloft, "only you and me and the car will stay active while Kathy freezes up with everybody else."

David looked across at his wife and then back at Richard. "You think she won't pick up on the car being active? I mean, she will be in contact with it."

Richard shrugged and held his hands palms up in front of his brother. "Dave, I don't know. Your guess is as good as mine. I mean, none of this makes any sense at all anyway."

"Do we *need* Kathy to be frozen? If we don't then we're through right here. We don't have to use the tape again."

"Well," Richard said, drawing the word out. "It would be better. She'd have a better chance, is what I mean. Dave, what you have to understand is, nothing is guaranteed. The alternative road is little more than a dirt track-" He pointed up the road to a distant left turn sign partly concealed by foliage and trees. "-and it'll be a bumpy ride. I'd prefer it if we could get her into hospital without bouncing her around too much. But even then..." He let his voice trail off and looked across at his patient.

David looked up at the sky and then down at the ground. The sun was getting dangerously low, its shadow almost across the road and into the long grass. "Well, whatever we decide to do, we're going to have to do it now." He drew in a deep breath and said, "Okay, let's do it."

Richard got into the car and moved it across to where the shadow was about to leave the blacktop. Then he and David carefully lifted Kathy's prone body and shuffled her into the rear seat. By this time, it was dusk.

David looked down at the road. The shadow had disappeared.

"Jesus Christ," he said, "It's gone."

Richard ran around the car. "No, it's in the bushes."

"I'm here and everything feels normal." He turned the key in the ignition and, as David ran around to the other side, the Toyota's engine burst into life. "Sounds good," he said, and released the brake.

As they pulled out onto the street, David noticed that the darkness had come back exactly where it had been before when he had looked out of the window. He had wondered if the Monitor thing simply returned to wherever it lived each time tape was removed but that didn't seem to be the case.

It was here. And it was here because *they* were here.

Richard swerved around a white pick-up making a left onto Birch Street. "This is weird," he said, unable to keep the chuckle out of his voice.

"Just take it easy," David said. "I have no idea what happens if we hit something."

They drove along Main Street and turned off onto the road that led to David's car. As they drove, David watched out of the back window and saw that the blackness had now evolved into the funnel shape, and something behind it seemed to be pushing the funnel out of shape in an attempt to break free. He crouched down and tried to see how far it went up into the sky. It went up as far as he could see, and that was high.

Whatever the Monitor was, it was big.

* * *

They reached the Oldsmobile in no time at all, but even that didn't seem quick enough for David.

He had been watching out of the back window all the way and he was sure that the funnel had now switched direction: it was definitely heading out of town the same way as they were traveling.

"Jesus, what a mess," Richard muttered as he pulled up alongside the wrecked car. He pulled on the brake and lifted the basket from the back.

"What do we do now?" David asked as he got out of the car.

Richard was already out and trotting across to Kathy's body.

"Well, I have to take a look at the wounds before you pull off the tape again," Richard answered, "then I guess we have to join real time, do what we can, and drive her to the hospital." He looked around at David. "Can we put her in the car and freeze her, and still be able to use the car?"

David shrugged. He glanced back and saw the blackness. It was towering over the road, bulging and throbbing. A wind had gotten up and was making it hard to breathe.

He looked back at Richard's face. "I don't know. Maybe. Maybe I have to be holding onto things for them to work... or at least holding onto someone else that's holding onto them. Maybe it only works through live matter and not through inert matter. That way we'll be okay."

"So long as Dormammu over there doesn't beam down and flatten us all," Richard said nodding to the shape down the road and towering over the trees.

"What's there to lose?" David asked.

"Well, don't let's think about that."

He leaned over Kathy and chewed his lip.

A few seconds later, he stood up and turned to David. "Okay," he said, "I don't think she's dead."

David breathed a sigh of relief.

"But we won't know that for sure until we join the real world. I can't even tell if she's breathing.

"Looks to me as though she's punctured her jugular."

"Oh, Christ," said David.

"No, it could be worse," Richard said. "If she'd got her carotid arteries she'd have bled to death in seconds." He looked down at her. "She's not in good shape, Dave... that much you should know. But maybe — just maybe — we're going to pull her through."

"What do you want me to do?"

He slid behind the wheel, started it up and pulled it onto the grass. "Okay," he said, leaning out of the window, "do your stuff."

David glanced back along the road towards town and moved across alongside Richard and the car. Then he placed the piece of dashboard on top of a bush which showed the faint sign of sunlight and shadow. He pulled the roll of tape out of his pocket and picked at a corner. When the tape came free, he pulled. The piece came off in his hand leaving only the circular spool. He looked at Richard.

"No second chances," he said as he bent down to the dashboard.

Richard nodded and placed his hand on his brother's neck.

David held the piece of tape in his right hand, making sure he was in a position to place it one-handed, and then took hold of the car door. Then he placed the tape.

A wind came up from nowhere.

Richard shouted, "Get in the car."

David ran around to the passenger side, relieved to hear the engine was still running, and pulled open the door. As he did, he looked back towards town. "Oh God."

"Get in the fucking car."

"We're not going to do it."

"Get *in*!" Richard shouted.

The rip was back again, pulling apart even as he watched. Black gas was pouring out and forming into the thing that he saw earlier. And it seemed to be doing it faster.

David slid into the moving car and slammed the door.

The Toyota's rear wheels screamed on the blacktop and the car shot off away from town.

David turned in his seat to see if Kathy was okay and then looked out of the rear window.

Tendrils of blackness interspersed with stars and milky swirls were snaking along the road towards them.

Richard had already reached the left turn and he

Lonesome Roads

span the wheel sending the car bouncing onto a gravel and soil pathway that was barely wide enough for a bicycle let alone an automobile. A little way down the road in front of them, a delivery truck was poised, frozen in time, its vacant-eyed driver staring sightlessly right at them.

David looked across at his brother. Without taking his eyes off the pathway ahead of them, Richard nodded. "I know," he said, "another half-minute and that guy would have been frozen right over the entrance."

David looked back through the window.

Somewhere behind them, over the trees on the road they had just left, a crack of thunder hammered out. Richard hunched his shoulders. The windshield shattered into a mosaic of spidery cracks and the back window blew out completely.

"Something isn't happy," David said as he watched his brother negotiate the car along the pathway.

"Can you see it?"

David shook his head.

All that he could see out of the rear window frame was tree branches. But the air was darkening. The only difference was that the darkness seemed to be spreading upwards from somewhere on the original road. "I think it must still be forming itself."

"Let's hope it takes its time."

"Amen to that."

Richard held out his hand. "Reach into the side pocket and hand me that wrench."

David looked down into the pocket and saw the wrench, but when he put his hand on it the thing wouldn't move. And it felt like a piece of porous sponge.

"It's no go with the wrench."

"Shit." Holding the wheel tightly with his left hand, Richard clenched his right hand into a fist and smashed it into the windshield. The glass broke into shards, a couple falling inside but most skidding onto the hood and off onto the path. He pushed the remaining pieces of glass free and then looked at his hand. It was bleeding around the knuckles and between the thumb and forefinger.

"That hurt," Richard said.

He span on the wheel and narrowly missed a wooden gatepost sitting at a drunken angle. The Toyota shot through the opening onto a concrete driveway that gave onto farm buildings. They passed a woman frozen in the act of helping a man load a roll of what looked like carpet over the tailgate of a Chevy flatback truck, the doors open wide like ears.

"Jim and Marge Connelly," Richard said, his eyes narrowed against the rush of wind in his face.

He turned the wheel in front of the farmhouse building and aimed for a narrow driveway that led onto another track. At the end of the track, David could see, was another blacktop. He could see cars, a couple of trucks and a bus, looking as though they were just parked on the road.

David looked back. The tendrils of blackness were snaking through the trees, wrapping themselves around branches momentarily and then breaking free to continue on their way.

"I think it's looking for us," David said over the wind that was buffeting them and taking their breath.

Richard didn't respond.

He pulled out onto the blacktop and David saw a sign a little way ahead, a left turn signposted **Forest Plains 3 miles**.

Once they were on the road, David looked across behind Richard and out of the back window. He could see the path they had just come down, leading up to a group of farm buildings — where he knew that Jim and Marge Connelly were still 'loading' a roll of carpet into a Chevy flatback — and beyond that the dirt-track that led away from their farm, past a grove of trees and back onto the original road where David's car sat. But something else also sat on that road, and now David could see it.

Lonesome Roads

Above the trees, which acted as almost a green, frilly hem on its black-as-night dress, towered something that resembled an upside-down twister. The part nearest the ground was bloated, thick black legs crooked out and straddling what must be the roadway, while the top end... well, David couldn't see the top.

The thing spiraled up into the sky further than David could see. About mid-way up the narrowing stem, a huge black blob was writhing from side to side. All around it, black smoke seemed to be swirling and billowing and, in the smoke, tiny pin-pricks of light twinkled. At either side of the shape, the sky seemed to be pulled back and even compressed... like a drawing of a sky on a canvas which had been punctured from behind and something forced through.

Another crack of thunder echoed and both Richard and David hunched up, half-expecting more glass to explode around them.

Ribbons of blackness were now twirling from the thing on the road, curling around the grove of trees in the distance in such numbers that the trees were now being replaced with solid black. Several of these ribbons were also moving around the farm buildings. One or two had extended themselves onto the road behind them. A couple more were even now moving across the fields on their left towards the fencing alongside the road... moving like fingers from some enormous hand, searching for something.

Just like 'The Hand From Beyond', David thought. Only he didn't think that this particular hand aimed to be as benevolent as its four-color counterpart in the long-ago pages of his *Strange Adventures* comicbook.

More thunder sounded and David saw the blob halfway up the column twirl around, elongate itself in their direction, and then stop.

"Shit!" David said.

"What is it?"

David watched as the entire column started to contract in on itself, compounding the hand-comparisons by seemingly clenching itself into a fist shape. Then it started to move. The thing was heading back into Forest Plains. Did it know where they were heading?

Richard turned the wheel and the Toyota careered across the road between a Ford Mercury and a Plymouth station wagon, narrowly missing the Plymouth's grill. "I have no idea why I'm indicating," Richard said as they passed the statue of a man in gaudily colored running shirt and shorts, the tip of his left foot on the sidewalk and his other leg arched up so that the knee almost touched his stomach.

"I think we may have trouble."

Richard nodded. "Like?"

"The thing is headed back into town on the other road."

Richard nodded. "The hospital is on this side of town. We'll do it."

Both of them could now see the Monitor towering in the air right in front of them, about a mile, maybe a mile and a half, away.

The black blob part of the column — the thing's head, David assumed — seemed to be stretching itself towards them, the piece above it swirling like some enormous conical hat tapering into the clouds.

The wind through the broken windshield was taking their breath away.

A sign came up on the right.

HOSPITAL
DRIVE CAREFULLY

Richard swung the wheel hard to the right. "Hold on," he shouted above the wind.

The Toyota skidded behind a red sedan and mounted the sidewalk. Richard kept the car going straight but the hospital entrance on the right was coming up too fast. They both saw the ambulance at the same time.

"I'm going to have to overshoot and pull around it,"

Lonesome Roads

Richard announced.

David nodded.

"Hold on."

He swung the wheel hard, slamming the brakes on, and pulled into the turning area. As they turned, the door behind Richard swung open, hit the small wall at the entrance, smashed and broke off. The door skittered along the sidewalk, narrowly missing a woman frozen in the act of walking, bounced off a roadsign, and skidded to a halt in the middle of the road.

David had instinctively reached over the back of his seat to hold onto his wife to stop her falling out of the car. As he had done so, he had dropped the dashboard on top of her.

He managed to keep Kathy in the car.

But the dashboard was now bouncing end over end across the road.

Richard pulled the car up in front of the hospital entrance behind an ambulance and pulled on the handbrake. He was starting to speak but David was already out of the car, running back the way they had just come.

Black finger-ribbons were now arcing across the road, some twirling themselves around roadsigns and checking the stationary cars, others already wrapping themselves around the buildings, caressing them for brief seconds and then moving on.

David reached the road and glanced to his right.

All he could see was blackness.

A huge dark shape was edging its way along towards him, enormous spindly legs — or elongated fingers — seeming to engulf everything on either side of the road.

Behind him, David heard Richard's voice. He was shouting something. He didn't turn around.

Dodging around a green Mustang, David ran across the blacktop. A black ribbon swirled in front of him and, instinctively, he jumped across it and kept running.

The dashboard was right ahead of him, lying on the

road a few yards in front of a Buick sedan that was more rust than brown. He could only thank whatever gods ruled the world that the thing had not actually skidded under a car. Another few steps...

Richard shouted again, more like a scream this time.

Thunder rolled and kept rolling, growing louder.

David was aware of a solid and all-engulfing blackness coming towards him on his right.

He bent down, shouting his wife's name as loud as he could, and lifted the dashboard from the road. Then he turned to his left and started running in the direction of the oncoming traffic.

A thick black finger-ribbon passed him by on the right and started to turn in towards him.

He fingered the edge of tape, mentally cursing.

The ribbon had stopped right in front of him, about fifty yards away, curling itself across the road so that he could only run into it. Behind him, more thunder split the heavens.

He got a corner of tape up.

Another finger-ribbon was coming at him from the left.

He pulled.

The tape came free.

The thunder stopped.

A car horn blared behind him and he dodged to the left. The brown and rust Buick shot past on his right, swerving into the inside lane and blocking the path of a Mercury Capri. He heard the dull crunch of metal and someone swearing.

A bus that was now heading towards him slammed its brakes on, the driver's face a mixture of surprise and horror, his arms held rigidly in front of him on the steering wheel.

David sidestepped the bus and saw a Lincoln, black hood and black windows, swerve to its left catching the rear of the bus.

He looked down the road and saw a truck heading up the slow lane but not going particularly slowly. It was going to hit him.

On his right, the bus was grinding to a halt, the Lincoln locked into its rear wheel arch.

Over on the other side of the road, the Buick was plowing through a collection of trashcans and heading towards a Realtor's office. He could see people through the window rushing out of the way.

Somewhere behind him, a pickup truck had hit the door of the Toyota and was screeching across four lanes of traffic.

Horns blared all around him. But there was no thunder.

David closed his eyes and jumped for the side of the road.

A sharp pain hit him in his right ankle and he felt something *twang!* in his left upper thigh just before he hit the sidewalk in a heap. He rolled over a couple of times and then came to a stop against a concrete wall. He waited, eyes closed, for car tires to run across him, squeeze his face like a grape, but there was only noise and shouting. Then he felt something in his side pocket. When he opened his eyes, Uncle Alan smiled down at him.

"Take it easy, big guy," Uncle Alan said. He was smiling and trying to reach into David's pocket.

David shook his head. There were a lot of other people standing just behind Uncle Alan, all of them smiling down at him... some of them strangely familiar.

"No," David said, and he placed a hand on his pocket.

The last thing he heard when he closed his eyes again was more screeching, more car horns, more crunching of metal and several voice snapshots. He was both pleased and a little disappointed that he didn't recognize any of them.

Then, though there was still no thunder, blackness engulfed him.

* * *

The sound of voices scared the blackness away.

Muted voices, distant telephones ringing, hollow and echoing announcements, bells and buzzers.

David opened his eyes and squinted at the light. It was coming from a window, its blinds horizontal.

He moved his arms and immediately felt pain in his side and his chest.

He was lying in a bed. Across the room, Richard was stretched out on a sofa, sound asleep. On the chair next to the sofa, David could see the shirt and pants he had been wearing, neatly arranged and folded.

He opened his mouth and felt strings of saliva stretch and break. His mouth tasted foul. He suspected it smelled even worse.

"Rich?"

Even speaking hurt his chest.

He closed his eyes and tried again. "Rich!"

There was a sound of movement and when he opened his eyes again, Richard was standing by the bed, bent over and holding his stomach, his right hand encased in a bandage. But he was smiling.

"How you doing, big brother?" Richard asked.

"You tell me."

Richard nodded. "Your ankle is smashed and in plaster. Two broken ribs — you'll discover you're strapped up tighter than Im Ho Tep and a bad case of concussion." He pointed at David's head. "You've got a lump topside that'll keep you flat for two weeks."

"But Kathy's fine."

David felt tears well up in his eyes and his throat constricted.

"How... how are *you*?" he said, holding back the emotion.

"Bruised and battered, but otherwise fine." He leaned against the bed. "The car's a total wreck. The ambulance I pulled up behind when everything started up again... it was reversing. It shunted me almost clear out of the parking area." He laughed.

"But Kathy's fine?"

Richard started to nod and then winced in pain. "Absolutely. She lost a lot of blood but she's been transfused and treated for concussion. She'll be out in a couple of weeks. Same time as you.

"The only thing we have to worry about is the police want to talk to us about recklessness. Reckless parking in a restricted area for me and, for you, reckless walking... particularly across a busy road. The officer asked me if my brother had always been an irresponsible asshole. No prizes for guessing my response."

David looked across at his clothes and then to the table next to them. He could see a small pile of objects, the topmost being a roll of Scotch tape. His eyes widened as he suddenly recalled seeing Uncle Alan.

Richard frowned and turned to see what his brother was looking at. Then he laughed. "That's from me, I'm afraid," he said. Seems the other one was all used up." Richard pulled something from his pocket. "But I held onto it for you," he said, holding an empty spool up high so that David could see it. "Call it a memento." Richard turned it over in his hand. "When they brought you in, you'd jammed your hand into your pants pocket. You were holding on to it like your whole life depended on it."

Even from the bed, David could see that a series of small symbols had been drawn around the circumference of the spool. He wondered if the power had been in the spool all along and not in the tape. If that were the case, then perhaps winding the fresh roll onto the old spool...

Thunder rolled somewhere off in the distance. David's mouth opened in horror but Richard reached over and held onto his brother's hand. "It's okay," he said. "It's just a storm. A *real* storm."

David nodded and closed his eyes. "It'll be good for the garden," he muttered. And even as he was still only drifting off to sleep, the dream started.

He was back at Bentley Grange, with Kathy... and he knew Uncle Alan was there — somewhere — but they hadn't been able to find him, even though he and Kathy had looked everywhere.

Outside in the garden the statues were still there. He knew this even though he could not see them from where he was sitting.

Somewhere in the distance, thunder was rolling here too.

Dust sheets covered all of the furniture and the room was silent. Over near the windows, where she had been looking out onto the chalk-marked garden, David's mother turned around and tried to give her son a reassuring smile. Next to her, David's father was holding onto her tightly.

"He'll be here soon," his mother said, unable to keep the nervousness out of her voice. "You must rest."

Then she turned away and looked out of the window at the gathering darkness.

"But you're..." David could not bring himself to tell his parents that they were dead. Instead, he said, "Who are we waiting for?"

There was no response.

"What exactly are those statues?" he asked.

Still nothing.

Then David asked his mother if anything was moving out there... but the thunder drowned out her reply. It sounded a whole lot nearer now.

When he looked down at his hands, David saw that he was holding a book. He turned it over and saw that the back cover seemed to be stained dark on the left-hand side.

He was not at all surprised when he saw the piece of tape.

Also available:-

razorblades

Short stories of visceral force from the pages of Raw Nerve magazine.
Full colour front and back jacket, A5, page count 150 Cover price £3.99 / $7.50
ISBN 0-9531468-0-4

Cutting edge fiction from Brian Wills, Peter Young, Tim Lebbon, Rhys Hughes, Julia Jones, Ian Girle, Andrew J Campbell, Gary Greenwood, Julia Jones, Paul Chidgey, Jane Fell, D F Stewart, Stuart Hughes, Douglas Brewis and Adrian Harding.

"...it makes a good visceral read, managing to be both gory and engaging, which is what you want from horror..." - SFX
"Marvellous... a real buttonholing quality from the off..." -Scavengers Scrapbook

Want to know more about RazorBlade Press? Visit us on

http://www.razorbladepress.com

Lonesome Roads

Faith in the Flesh

Two gripping novellas of mystery and imagination!

"*Faith in the Flesh*" consists of two novellas linked by a theme. The first novella "*The First Law*" is set during an unspecified war. It tells the story of a group of ship wreck survivors. When they land on a deserted island they think that their prayers have been answered, but nothing could be further from the truth.
"*From Bad Flesh*" the second novella is set in a civilisation brought to its knees by a plague. It charts the desperate journey of Gabe, as he goes in search of a cure, but discovers a terrible secret.
Both novellas have a terrifying narrative which makes the book gripping.
ISBN 0-9 531468-4-7. £4.99/$9.00

"...this book marks Lebbon out very much as an author to watch."
A ~ *SFX*

"Lebbon never disappoints. His consistently first rate stories crackle with invention and surprises galore." - *Simon Clark*

"...a superb read from beginning to end...Lebbon has both the talent and audacity to pull off some startling feats of literary world-building..." - *David Howe, Shivers*

Tim Lebbon

THE DREAMING POOL

"Wickedly Good" - Simon Clark

The story begins with Jack Bradley being called back to his home town of Caerphilly when his father is brutally murdered. Jack learns that the body was found at a child hood haunt, the Dreaming Pool, and soon has to confront not only a long buried secret, but also a conspiracy which leaves Jack not knowing who to trust.
£4.99/$9.00 ISBN 0-9 531468-7-1.

"A gritty slice of life, driving dialogue and no nonsense horror makes this one heck of a read...Wickedly good" - *Simon Clark*

"An impressive debut" B ~ *SFX*

GARY GREENWOOD

Introduction by Simon Clark